COMBINADO DEL ESTE

Mireya Robles

Victor's Story
Fort Chaffee, 1981

Translated by Susan Griffin
with the collaboration of the author

Order this book online at www.trafford.com
or email orders@trafford.com

Most Trafford titles are also available at major online book retailers.

Note for Librarians: A cataloguing record for this book is available from Library
and Archives Canada at www.collectionscanada.ca/amicus/index-e.html

Printed in Victoria, BC, Canada.

ISBN: 978-1-4269-2422-4 (Soft)

*We at Trafford believe that it is the responsibility of us all, as both individuals
and corporations, to make choices that are environmentally and socially sound.
You, in turn, are supporting this responsible conduct each time you purchase a
Trafford book, or make use of our publishing services. To find out how you are
helping, please visit www.trafford.com/responsiblepublishing.html*

*Our mission is to efficiently provide the world's finest, most comprehensive
book publishing service, enabling every author to experience success.
To find out how to publish your book, your way, and have it available
worldwide, visit us online at www.trafford.com*

Trafford rev. 01/25/2010

 www.trafford.com

North America & international
toll-free: 1 888 232 4444 (USA & Canada)
phone: 250 383 6864 ♦ fax: 812 355 4082

at six p.m., within the walls of my apartment, I begin to forget the tiredness I carried with me from my place of work; from the streets where I traffic in illegal goods to obtain bread for my sister, for my niece Yuny, for my wife Niurka who, for the last few months has lived with us along with her daughter Yardely; Niurka, old lady, will you draw a bath for me? come here, Yuny, how's my girl today, are you studying hard? know what, Yuny, if you're good, I'll take you out on Sunday; yes, Uncle Mede, I have been good and I'm going to be very good, and you'll take me, Uncle? yes, I'll take you, yes, of course I'll take you too Yardely, come here and give your Daddy a kiss; yes, Yardely, Daddy Mede loves you very much too; Mede! Mede! your bath's ready; I'm coming, Niurka; tell me, Toña, why do you worry like that? yes, sister, I know I must return early, don't get all worked up, sister, I'll be

back early; Daddy Mede, Daddy Mede, Yuny took my
doll, it's my doll; Uncle Mede, it's my doll and
Yardely wants to take it away from me; well, Yuny,
let Yardely have the doll because she's the
littlest; yes, Uncle Mede, but she'll break it;
the argument begins to wind down with a command
from Niurka: Yardely, give the doll to Yuny, right
now; the doll passes quickly from Yardely's hands
to Niurka's hands, to those of Yuny, and it all
ended up with Yardely's sobs, with the voluntary
banishment of Yuny to Toña's room, with Yuny's
drawn out laughter; the bath refreshes me, relaxes
me, I enjoy the comfort of my pyjamas; from my
room I call Niurka and she, wait, Mede, I'm busy;
but I don't have to wait long because Toña is
already here, as always, waiting on me, you can
be a real nuisance, brother, what is it that you
want, should I iron your trousers and must they
be these ones, Mede? can't you wear any of the
ones that are already ironed? ok, let's see, give
them here; now I'm dressed in my blue shirt and
my recently ironed jeans; on my way to the door
Niurka detains me with a kiss, Yardely with her
request for a kiss and Yuny with a request too,
but Yuny, as always, touches me, I always tell
myself that Yuny is a part of my skin, the vision
of my eyes; I move away after a last kiss to my
sister, with the decisive goodbye of a bird
escaping from winter, with the finality of a
condemned man taking leave of his cell mate; out
in the street, some of the neighbours greet me;
in my hand, the protest poems, I don't know
whether to take them to Alexis so that she can
give them to her relations, Members of the
Community, who are about to arrive from the

United States, so that they can have them
published there; I laugh when I'm with Alexis,
she always says to me, imagine, Mede, how strange,
my relations, when they left, were called *gusanos*,
worms, and now, because they return with dollars
and leave dollars here, now they've taken to
calling them 'Members of the Community,' that
really is funny; how beautiful the night that has
fallen over the neighbourhood, with its melancholy,
its starry sky, that narrow brilliance; at the
bus stop on Route 10 I approach a woman about 35
years old, has the bus been long in coming? and
that's how I start my conversation and the bus's
delay gives me time to tell her how beautiful I
find her dark eyes, her slender figure, her fine
lips; we get onto the bus with its sign saying
Monte, we sit together and when I hear her
invitation, would you like to stop by my house a
while? I am almost overcome by the temptation,
but, no, madam, thank you, thank you, and I tell
myself that tonight nothing must distract me from
the need to reach Guanabacoa, it's better that I
take these to La China, it's better that I send
them with her relations; I get off at Virgen del
Camino to take Route 5, in the open doorway, La
China's surprise; Mede, what wind blew you here?
another problem with the law? well, no, no wind
blew me here, but yes, I do have a problem; yes,
I know, Mede, whenever you appear here it's to
find a solution; listen, China, my love, I have a
lot of work and I can't come, you know what it's
like to travel from El Vedado to here? is it your
work or is it your wife who won't let you leave
your house? you know that no-one, not my wife,
not anyone, rules me; ok, ok, let's drop it, what

do you want of me; well, it has to do with this
notebook, look; La China starts paging through
the poems, hey! we're prospering, now we've got a
typewriter? it's not prosperity, China, it's a
friend's typewriter, he types them up for me; you
with all your friends always, but tell me, what
do you want to do with these poems? I want to
leave the notebook with you, China, look after
them, no-one better than you knows the problems I
have with the law; if they search my house, I'll
be arrested, I was thinking that when your sister
comes from El Norte she can take them for me? but
what do you want her to take them for? they can
be published there, China, there they can publish
them; I keep quiet watching her decide, my eyes
follow the notebook in her hand, she holds it out
to me; keep it, Mede, when my sister comes, we'll
talk again; and now she looks at me attentively:
and you're still persisting with your devotion to
books, the books that kept us apart? well, China,
books are my life, why bring up the past? does it
hurt you to remember because I'm still the only
woman for you? don't make life difficult, if you
were the only woman for me I would have come back
to you; time will be our witness, Mede, time will
tell; I kept quiet so as not to hurt China, I no
longer feel anything for her; Mede, come with me,
why don't you come with me to my goddaughter's
birthday in Havana Centre? she's my *ahijada*, my
goddaughter in the Afro-Cuban religion, the one
who was here when I had the drums played for
Changó; and it comes to me quickly, our common
ground, our *Santería*, *Obatalá*, the main saint;
Eleguá, with whom the ceremonies are performed;
Changó, the warrior saint, dressed in red,

transformed through the necessity of hiding our
origins, into Saint Barbara; *Ochún*, who became
Our Lady of Charity; *Yemayá*, our ruler of the
seas, who became Our Lady of Regla; *Ogún*, warrior
saint, lord of iron; *Oyansa*, mistress of the
cemetery; *Sojuano*, our beloved Saint Lazarus;
Algayú, Changó's father, transformed into Saint
Michael; when I met you, China, you were already
initiated into Santería as the daughter of an
African deity, I don't know what illness caused
you to do it, I can only imagine the animals,
goats, sheep, chickens, roosters, pigeons,
turtles, that disappeared in the ceremony, I
imagine you during the first stage, in the home
of the *babalao* who, with the help of the Board of
Orula, indicates which African deity you should
become the daughter of; I imagine you dressed in
white during the seven days on your throne and
then, already become *Iyabó*, wearing only white
for a year; I never knew the name given to you in
Santería, the one that came to you from the *itá*,
from the mat sprinkled with Cowrie shells; but we
navigated through the secrets of our myths,
through the strange language of our chants; La
China comes towards me dressed so elegantly now,
wearing the protection of her necklaces, remember,
China, how we insisted on the exactness of the
colours: Obatalá's is a white necklace; Eleguá's,
black and red; Changó's, red with white beads;
Ochún's, yellow; Yemayá's, blue; Ogún's, black;
Sojuano's, purple with white stripes; Oyansa's,
grey with ash coloured stripes; yes, China, of
course I'll stay for dinner; later, after freshly
perked coffee and two beers, we walked to the bus
stop to catch the Route 95 bus; we tired of

waiting and I followed La China's lead when she
unexpectedly flagged down a passing taxi and we
climbed in; I lit up a Popular cigarette so as to
better enjoy the beauty of the Vía Blanca, do you
want one, China? no, Mede, you know I always
smoke Aurora; we climbed the stairs of the old
building in Aguila Street, we walked along the
long corridor, I followed La China up to the
small door of the apartment packed with people;
there are a few children, as always in the
Santería celebrations; La China's ahijada lies
face down on the mat to greet her godmother, next
she picks up the maraca and starts playing it and
speaking in *Lucumí*; I watch from the sofa where
I'm sitting; the walls are decorated with
colourful cloths; the dish on the floor with
pesos which the participants have placed in it;
the soup tureens are well decorated; the saint
lives in the tureens and his secret is there; I
had a few beers and Habana Clubs; I danced a few
numbers; I saw La China disappear into one of the
rooms with her *ahijada* to carry out ceremonies in
honour of the saint, I spoke to a woman who
seemed pleasant amongst the smell of smoke and
the voice of José Valladares; Mede, I've finished
the ceremonies, it's already eleven o'clock, are
you coming home with me? no, China, I have to
work tomorrow; I felt her hand on my arm, holding
me back, don't be mean, will your wife hit you if
you arrive late? maybe, but I must go, come, give
me a kiss; I felt her kiss on my lips and her
promise: Mede, come by my house tomorrow, I've
got something good saved for you; awaiting me in
the street were fresh air, a blue sky, a beautiful
night that brings memories of La China, her slim

figure that drove me crazy so many nights and
today, China, you're a dear, you're all those
pleasures that fade into forgetfulness; I walk
along Reina towards the El Parque de la
Fraternidad; arriving at the park I recognize a
woman with whom I have spoken on a number of
occasions, I walk with her, we arrive at her
house near the train station; I accept her
invitation, she takes out a bottle of Caney, we
have a few drinks, while the night advances we
make love; then it's time for me to go, while I
wait at the bus stop, I think how this woman's
body could drive anyone crazy; hey! citizen! your
ID! I made out the police car in front of me, the
shouts of the cop behind the steering wheel; the
pistol that another cop aims at me and his shouts,
up against the wall! but sir, this is no way to
treat a citizen; shut your mouth unless you want
a mouthful of my fist; don't even try it, don't
throw any punches at me because, see, I also have
my two fists; oh! so you think you're a hero? I
don't think I'm a hero but you have no right to
beat me; I have no right to beat you? let's see,
what's that in your hand; and now the driver's
voice resounds in the night, hey, put him in the
car, let's see how brave he is when he gets to
the station; by the time I got into the patrol
car I had already been searched from head to toe,
they had taken my ID and the notebook; I felt the
car start, the movement of the car towards the
Police Station, my presence at the desk; look,
sergeant, I've brought you a hero; oh, so you've
brought me a real fighter? wait, I'll take care
of this one; almost immediately the cop comes up
to me with the notebook open in his hand, my

friend, this is something I can't forgive you
for; I felt the blow in my stomach, I doubled
over with the pain, I felt them beating me
savagely; some policemen approach and the cop
starts reading them the poems; while I hear the
words I wrote in his voice, I feel the violence
of the police; I fell under their blows, I feel
their kicks covering every inch of my body; the
cop hauls me up: bastard, son of a bitch, I'll
teach you to bad mouth this revolution; the
sergeant's shouts reach me: this ungrateful
bastard from his mother's cunt, after all we've
done for him and look at the shit he writes;
everything began to fade, I saw nothing more; I
awoke lying on the floor of a dark cell; I try to
get up, the pain won't let me move, I cannot
control my moaning; the prisoner who is lying on
his cement bed turns to me: hey, you, what
happened, did you mess with the big boys? I
battle to adjust to the darkness, I find simple
words difficult: nothing, I'm in the shit;
another prisoner starts passing comments, looks
like they've messed you up, friend, looks like
they've dropped you like a sack of potatoes, what
happened to you? through the laughter of many I
hear myself say, I already said nothing happened,
a small problem; I ignored the laughter, I felt
the pain burning me deeply, I was revolted to be
in that cell, I felt the pages of the notebook
losing themselves for always like a kite carried
by the wind; I remembered the exact moment in
which I decided to pay 200 pesos to have those
verses typed up; Ugly's voice brought me back to
the reality of the cell, I looked at his white
hair, his extremely short stature, while he told

his story; this is what you call bad luck, I
check out the drunk in the bar, I push him, I
take his watch and forty pesos and at that moment
three men arrive, they rob me of what I've taken
from the drunk plus what I have, I set off at a
run and a little later the police haul me out of
my house because they found the drunk naked and
with my ID next to him; I stop listening to the
conversation, I measure my pain, I ask myself
which bone is broken, I start screaming, nobody
answers, except one prisoner, listen, you, let
people sleep; another prisoner helps me sit on
the cement bed; a cop brings a drunk and throws
him into the cell, who's shouting? I am,
combatiente; this is no time to be shouting the
place down; my whole body hurts, I need to see
the doctor; oh, yes, it's the little worm, what
I'll give you is another round of beating, you
don't play with us, *gusano* from your mother's
cunt; when I see him move away, a prisoner asks
me, oh, you're here because you're a *gusano*?
compadre, not even I know what to call the shit
I'm in; another protests, ok, ok, let's drop it
now and get some sleep, in a little while the
interrogations start; I make out the smell of
urine, of excretion, the sight of the drunk
they've just brought taking off his clothes as if
he were in his own home, preparing to sleep
completely naked; little by little I raise myself,
I peer at the corridor, I look at my own cell, I
see two men lying on the same bed, I look out
again, I see the cop with another prisoner; he
opens the cell next door, the prisoner enters;
the cop calls my name, reading it from a piece of
paper he holds, he opens the gate, I leave, he

directs me down the corridor to the door; my
escort knocks on the door; a tall man, with skin
burnt by the sun, dressed in a military uniform,
wearing the stripes of a lieutenant appears;
here's the detainee, lieutenant; the cop holds a
tight salute; permission to leave, lieutenant?
yes, you may leave, but don't go far, I might
have work for you; permission to retire; granted!
and now, move, you, if you don't want me to make
you move, you've fucked up my sleep; I entered a
well lit office, with a bureau, two chairs, a
sofa, various posters bearing the faces of
revolutionary figures on the walls; the light
tormented me, my body ached; I felt my lip
swelling, I could hardly open my left eye, I
walked with difficulty; the official pointed to
a chair, listen, you, sit; I managed to sit with
some effort, I looked straight at the official;
so you're Mede? I kept looking at him, without
answering; are you deaf? can't you hear that I'm
talking to you? yes, I'm Mede, and I was surprised
how weak my voice sounded; so this notebook is
yours? it's better that you tell the truth because
it's in your interest to do so; what else can I
tell you? the notebook is mine; questions started
to rain down, names, names, names and more names,
and I, repeatedly, I don't know who they are, I
know nothing about them; and your address, what
is your address? I gave an address in Santos
Suárez instead of mine because I can't allow them
to go to my house and find things there that can
be used against me; the interrogation ended in
the morning; I returned along the corridors, my
cell was full, there was nowhere for me to sit;
so, my friend, how did it go there? said the one

who was lying on the stone bed next to the door; these people with all their fucking around won't leave me in peace, I replied; a young prisoner shouts at the person who now occupies the bed where hours before I had sat, listen, *compa*, get off that bed, its owner is here, and starts to shove the man who was lying there and who is now protesting, but brother, let me sleep, you can't even get some sleep in this filthy cell, but the young prisoner insisted, get up, this isn't an hotel, or you would have been here sooner; I watched the man get up, I watched him find a spot on the floor while I lay myself down on the stone bed; thanks, *paisano*, I said to the young prisoner; you're welcome, my friend; I slept for I don't know how long, until the voices of two men fighting each other over a bed woke me; wait until we get to Combinado Prison, there I'll make you my woman; hey, but look at her, after she lost it in the other bed, look how she is blustering; they continued arguing in the strange language that is used in the street; various attempts to get their hands on each other are frustrated because the others intervened; everything began calming down; a prisoner started telling me how he was caught as he was leaving the occupied house he was robbing; I told him about my situation, I heard him tell me, listen, you're in big shit, not even the Chinese doctor can save you; the other prisoners started telling their stories, I was caught with a car full of rolls of material; they arrested me for carrying a 38; and me because I was drunk in the street; and me for knifing someone in the Cayo Hueso neighbourhood, I sent him straight to hospital;

we were arrested for causing a public scandal,
he's active and I'm passive and they caught us
doing it on the stairs of a building; I catch the
smell of sweat, of the shit that one of the
prisoners is voiding in the cell at this moment;
Orlando says that he's here for illegal vending,
Orlando, who will be with me through the most
difficult moments of this long journey as a
prisoner; the changing of the guard brings a roll
call, one soldier and three officials open the
bars and order us out into the corridor; now
we're all out, but an official enters the cell
with a flashlight to ensure that nobody stays
behind; they start to call out names and, as each
one hears his name, he goes back into the cell,
the investigator in charge of my case approaches;
stay outside because we have a lot to talk about;
once again I walk along the long passage to the
door that I already know; I read the sign:
Investigations, I entered the same office, sat
down, and in front of me the official repeated
the questions, I answered the same; the
interrogation ended with a shout: enough! enough
of your lies, I have made enquiries, you don't
live at that address, but I'm going to make you
talk until you spill your guts if you don't
cooperate; I don't know anything about what you
want me to say; oh, so you're still denying it,
look, I'm going to take you back to your cell so
that you can get your memory back, it seems that
the beating made you lose your memory; I'm still
in pain, my head is bursting, I can hardly get up,
I have to do something, I stand, I fall to the
floor, if they believe I've fainted they'll take
me to the hospital; I hear the official's voice,

get up off the floor and stop pretending, can't you hear, or do you want me to get you up; I stayed on the floor, aware of my painful swollen eyelid, immobile, aware of my aching lip, of the pain boring through my body; I felt the lieutenant's footsteps, I felt him open the door, guard! guard! I thought that the guard would come and beat me again, I stayed limp; the footsteps that came from the passage stopped in front of me, yes, sir? get ready to take this detainee to the hospital, he's fainted; yes, lieutenant, at once, permission to leave; permission granted; I was alone once more with the official, I felt him crouch down to take my pulse, he stopped and spoke to himself, aloud: these elements never learn their lesson; two men picked me up, one by my feet, the other by my shoulders, I felt them lift me, I heard the voice of a guard, this one was beaten up good and they say his case is serious, and the other, these young people don't learn, the other day I arrested one for fighting, they released him, and two days later I caught him again with American cigarettes and, you know, he's off to prison; now we're in the street, another voice, open the rear door so that we can throw him in; I felt myself thrown onto the floor at the back of the car; as soon as we began moving I felt calmer, I opened my good eye, but soon the potholes made me bounce on the floor, I began moaning loudly until the car stopped; one of the escorts tried to open the rear door, but couldn't; Carlos, take the security lock off this door; the other obeyed without replying; comrade! bring me a stretcher! the escort and a nurse place me on the stretcher, everything spins round

me; the world begins disappearing, everything
goes dark, I don't know for how long; upon waking
the first thing I feel is a pain in my arm;
they've given me a drip; my left eye is bandaged;
I'm surrounded by a doctor, a nurse, a guard; the
doctor speaks to me, how are you feeling? not so
good, doctor, my whole body hurts; tell me, young
man, what happened to you? the police beat me up
this morning; the escort doesn't allow me to
finish: he was looking for trouble by trying to
be clever and showing disrespect; the doctor
stares at him and then leaves; the doctor is
dark, tall, about thirty years old; the nurse is
about twenty, she takes my blood pressure, writes
something on a piece of paper, and leaves; I'm
left alone with the soldier; *combatiente*, what
hospital is this? it's the Emergency Hospital;
what time is it about? it's four in the afternoon
and you were lucky that they allowed you to check
in, don't try one of your tricks here because
I'll shoot you; I'd rather be dead than to live
like you; stop talking shit if you don't want a
good hiding; do what you want, it's the truth;
you're only safe because we're here, if we were
at the Station I'd make you eat your words; I
kept quiet, I started thinking about Niurka, she
will think that I'm with some woman, my sister
worries me, every time I've had a problem, she
gets very sick, I can't warn my family, no-one
knows that I'm here; the nurse arrives, miss, let
me go to the toilet; no, you can't get off that
bed, let me give you a bedpan, if you need me,
push the buzzer; in my ward there were two more
beds, two old men it seemed, sleeping; now the
lady with the tray appears, bringing the food, I

didn't want to eat; the escort left when his
relief arrived; at ten o'clock that night they
take out my drip; at eleven a nurse aid arrived,
dressed in pink; I accept a cigarette from her,
we chat until she leaves the ward; my head no
longer hurts, I feel better, they can't send me
to Combinado Prison, or to Security, just like
that, so easily, I walk to the bathroom to
familiarise myself with the layout; in the
bathroom I find a window which looks out onto a
flat roof belonging to the hospital, a smaller
building; my escort fell asleep, he looked
exhausted; I went out into the corridor without
making a sound; this half open door may solve my
clothes problem; I pushed it, no one was there, I
took a white shirt and a pair of white trousers;
upon re-opening the door, I come face to face
with a woman; what are you doing in there? I
start running down the corridor, towards the
stairs, I can hear the woman's shouts: a thief, a
thief; on the ground floor, a man, I push him;
I'm in a big hall, I want to reach the glass door,
I can't open it, the escort grabbed me by the
shirt, a cop gets me in an armlock; two other
cops start yelling obscenities at me, I listen in
silence; at the Station, they get ready to beat
me up but an official on duty stops them; they
take me to the cell, it's around two in the
morning, I chat to those I know; one of the women
in the cell next door starts screaming obscenities;
another shouts at her, shut up, whore, when we
get to Nuevo Amanecer we'll see if you still feel
like shouting; I fell asleep on my stone bed, the
roll call wakes me; we went out, we entered again,
someone starts to call out the names on a list, I

hear my name; they took us out into the corridor;
they cuffed me; they put me into a car built like
a cage along with other detainees; the journey
was short, very short; they take us out of the
cage, we were in the Havana Audience Hall; I
asked myself what I was doing there as I hadn't
even been charged; they took us to the second
floor, to the third assembly room; the black
cassocks envelope the bodies of the speakers;
there are three older men and one woman who acts
as a secretary in the assembly hall; they begin
reading a common indictment for eight accused,
all young; the charge of antisocial behaviour
heads the list of accusations; we are accused by
a military man with the rank of official that I
see for the first time; he is of medium height,
dark, with a body deformed by fat; I see the
national emblem, the flag; the secretary reads on
endlessly, accusations that have nothing to do
with me; the prosecutor takes the floor, he
prepares to launch into a speech: comrades, we
can't sit back and ignore these antisocial
delinquents, these pariah that disturb the order
of our society; we must be exacting as this
revolution has put us here as representatives of
our country's laws; it's the defense attorney's
turn: gentlemen, comrades, I ask clemency for my
defendants; they're young and lack experience,
they are the youth that we should build up, not
destroy; we must see justice done, if my
defendants are actually guilty of everything they
have been accused of, where is the proof? the
judge, with a smack of his gavel, interrupted the
words of the defense attorney, enough! the
prosecutor supported him, let's deliberate; they

conversed amongst themselves; we, the accused, remained silent; the judges finished deliberating, the prosecutor declared: we have determined that the accused are guilty of infringing Article 1254 of the Civil Defense Code passed by the Ministry of Justice in the year 1978; as such, given that we consider the accused to be a grave danger to society, we sentence them to four years of incarceration in a penitentiary, this is my final word; the tribunal gets ready to withdraw without hearing our testimony; I stopped them, Your Honours, I would like you to listen to my views on the injustice that you have just perpetrated; it is obvious that no-one present in this hall today has ever been in a penitentiary, where man is slowly transformed into an animal, is corrupted, loses his vision of the future, lays himself open each day to unexpected death; if any one of you were to spend 72 hours in a prison, you would resign from the posts that you occupy today; with great indignation they ordered me to keep quiet; in silence I listened as they extended my sentence by a further two years; we arrived at the Police Station; they distributed us throughout the different cells; now in mine, a prisoner asks me for a cigarette or the butt of one, I didn't have any, I hadn't smoked for hours, another prisoner offered me two butts so that I can twist them in newspaper to make a *breva* or a *tupamaro*; another prisoner asks me, *compa*, pass the *breva* this way so that I can take a drag, I'm going crazy; wait, I'm first, bursts out another prisoner; we pass the *breva* around and each take a few drags; lunch, which consists of a little cold corn meal, without lard or salt, arrives; by two in the afternoon

they had prepared the report on me, they were
sending me to Combinado del Este, a modern prison
in Havana; I thought I was lucky to be moved so
quickly; there is no hygiene in the Station,
there is nowhere to wash and the food consists of
a small ration of corn meal for lunch and again
for supper; some of those who will stay have
already spent more than two weeks in the Station;
in the lock-up car, we're packed in, those of us
who are sitting have to have someone sitting on
our legs; the heat becomes unbearable, some of us
take off our shirts; the lock-up car leaves to
arrive an hour later at Combinado; in its
beautiful setting, it can easily be mistaken for
a secondary school in the country, for a technical
school, without one being able to suspect from
outside the hell it contains; Combinado is made
up of various buildings, all modern; at the
entrance, a small house, next to it, a hut where
the families of the inmates meet on Visitors'
Days, after that the guard post and then,
Management where the inmates' documents are kept;
a series of offices, the officials' dining room
and their dormitories; next door, the soldiers'
barracks; further on there is a mechanics workshop
and then, the entrance to the factory, where the
prefabricated units used to construct buildings
and schools are made; the inmates work ten hours
a day for very low wages or for free in the
factory; upon leaving for work or when they
return, the inmates go through a very strict
search; on the outskirts of the prison there is
a farm where those with minor sentences work; at
the entrance to the prison, the cafeteria, for
visitors, where they sell cigarettes, sweets and

other items; the prison is made up of three four-story buildings; a kitchen, bakery and sweet factory; a hospital where inmates and women from Nuevo Amanecer are treated; the Visitors' Hall; the three buildings, simply numbered One, Two, Three; the doors are opened from an electronic board on each floor; each floor, which has a North wing and a South wing, is overseen by a guard who carries a telephone with which he calls the board to indicate the number of the cell which should be opened; but sometimes the prisoners open it with a good, hard pull, and it closes quickly, so quickly, as soon as a light on the board lights up and warns them; we're about eight hundred to a thousand prisoners; each cell is designed to hold 37 people and we're about eighty or a hundred prisoners; from five in the morning I hear the on your feet!; at six, roll call; breakfast follows; at eleven, lunch; at four, supper; at six or seven, last roll call of the day; at ten, silence is called; that day we got out of the lock-up car at Building Three; we lined up before the official on duty in the holding area, the one in charge of arrivals; there follows a blood test, photos of the new arrivals; we're seated on benches like those I sat on so many times in parks; fingerprints; they give us the cards that we will use in the prison, when we have a visitor or a physical exam, when a prisoner is missing from the cells, when the head count does not tally, they call us by the information on our card; the guard's voice: name, surname, date of birth, place of birth, number of times a prisoner, current address, height, father's name, mother's name; I'm passed into the holding area, the room is packed, some are seated, while others look for a place to lie down, the stink of urine, always the stink of urine and unbearable sweat; I begin recognizing prisoners; we chat about our situation; almost all of us are here for Dangerousness; conversation ceases, I retire to a corner of the floor, I think about my family, I think that my last days with them were wonderful; hey, *paisano*, don't you remember me? I look at him and try to remember, who can it be? I think I saw him in, ah, *compadre*, it's you; he asks me a question, so, did you carry on with the illegal trafficking? yes, I assure him, it's quite a lucrative business; what's new now? he asks again; nothing, I've been given a long stretch, four for Dangerousness and two for saying what I had to say; but my friend, how can you go and get yourself into such shit when you were living like a king? I've also got another four year sentence, I'm rotting here; we continue talking, a finger, from amongst a group, beckons to me, I recognise the voice of Orlando; brother, come here a moment; when I approach he starts talking to me, let's try and be placed together so that we can talk a little about outside; we chatted until they started calling us to give us a change of clothing: grey trousers; black, collarless shirt without buttons, closed up to the neck; they took our shoes and gave us sneakers; they gave me a crew cut; I want to wash, I need a bath but I have nothing to dry myself with, I ended up drying myself with my underpants; the prisoners start talking about bullying, that they'd kill, that they do it, that they don't do it; one prisoner bumped into another with whom he'd had problems; they argue, one wounds the other with a razor; the guards come to take them away, but before taking them, one of the guards beats up the prisoner who holds the razor, with a machete, he bears up under the blows without a whimper; in Indian file they take us to eat, hands behind our backs; rice, fish, bread; we devour everything as if it were the finest delicacy that ever existed; time for the head count; we make ourselves as comfortable as possible in the filthy cell; the guard asks if there are any homosexuals so that they can be put with the other homosexuals; no-one wanted to leave; I make myself comfortable in a corner, I think about the life that I have to lead, I think about the years that I have been sentenced to, I think about the five or ten years that they will sentence me to for a case that is still pending; with these thoughts I fall asleep; a desire to urinate woke me; it's so difficult to walk between the prisoners, the floor is packed, one prisoner piled on top of another, I find two inmates seated on the sink; I manage to go to sleep, at daybreak I awake with a start; everything happens behind bars; I wash my face, wait for the head count; breakfast: milk and bread; I learn that water is given three times, during breakfast, lunch and supper; the prisoners talk, many that are older than 40 are in prison for masturbating in public, for molesting boys and girls of two years old, of ten, of twelve years; one is in prison for molesting his three daughters, he continued defending his right to molest them because he had made them and he supported them; four days pass, I'm still in the holding area; I

receive my transfer to the second floor of the
same Building Three, it's night, they send me to
the North wing, cell 3203: Building Three, second
floor, cell three; I recognized the cell that I
was in for six months, after the sweep before the
Onceno Festival in 78; all the prisons in Havana
were packed, they had to send prisoners to the
country's interior; Combinado's cells were
crammed with up to 120 prisoners; that was the
year when the Law of Dangerousness was first
applied; in the cell I recognize China's brother,
detained for having a list of bets; we started
talking, we struck up, for the first time, a type
of friendship; he spoke to me about the street,
he spoke to me about the way to behave in the
prison; he gave me a cigarette; we were 82 in a
cell for 37 people, I managed to get ready for
sleep on a piece of cardboard along with another
prisoner in for pick-pocketing; the air is cold,
I feel it more intensely against the bars, I have
nothing to cover myself with; then in the morning,
I discovered that it was Visitors' Day for those
awaiting trial, I sent a message with a friend;
prisoners awaiting trial are allowed a visit
every 15 days; prisoners condemned to a maximum
of six years receive visits every 21 days; those
condemned to more than six years are allowed
visitors once a month; sad days pass by, more
than two weeks, my transfer to Building Number
One arrives, first floor; it's three in the
afternoon, on the way a little sun reaches me for
the first time since my incarceration; I see a
courtyard, a sports ground with a field for
soccer and football; the prison is surrounded by
three fences, two of eight metres, one a bit

smaller; the penitentiary is, on average, a block long and a block wide; every 50 meters there is a tower with a guard aiming a KM; the political prisoners are on the third and fourth floors of Building One; the foreign prisoners are in the South wing of the fourth floor; treatment is better in One, the food, a little more plentiful; they gave us a talk, they dispersed us; Papito el Choro, the pickpocket, and I are sent to a cell containing two religious types and another five people; one of these people, El Bemba, calls Papito and offers him a vacant bed; I started arguing for the bed, why should he give that bed to Papito when I arrived in the cell first? I want to give it to him because I know him; Raúl, a Jehovah's Witness, intervenes, *caballero*, don't argue over that bed because El Chinito is being released today; we calm down while waiting for an old Chinaman, about 80 years old, arrested for refusing to pay 90 pesos, to leave; in this cell there are three bunks, each with three beds; the two Jehovah's Witnesses and Bemba sleep in the first one; sleeping in the other bunk is a political prisoner, about 65 years old, who was put in with the ordinary prisoners where he spent three years, strangely enough, they accused him of being a bookie, he was caught along with 365 bookmakers in a sweep carried out by State Security when it was decided that bookmakers were counter revolutionaries; when the Government reached an agreement with the United States to release the political prisoners, many of these prisoners were sent to swell the numbers of ordinary prisoners; they opened the door for us; Raúl, the Jehovah's Witness, introduced me to the

others; Lázaro, short, stocky, about 30, also a
Jehovah's Witness, like Raúl a prisoner for
devoting himself to preaching; he points to a 23
year old youth, this is Roberto, they gave him
three years for Dangerousness; Bemba, 25, is
doing two for Dangerousness; Carlos, 38 years
old, keeps quiet and makes no mention of his
crime; the soldier, 24 years old, is doing four
for a robbery committed while doing his obligatory
Military Service; Papito the pickpocket came with
me from Building Three; we are the constituents
of cell 1115; the two Jehovah's Witnesses gave me
a sheet, a mattress, a towel and a pair of prison
trousers, and I thought, this is the difference
between the political prisoners and the ordinary
ones, these share what they have, the others even
take the clothes on your back; the Jehovah's
Witnesses carried on offering, Mede, take what
you need, take anything you need; you know, Mede,
you should know our Creator; but tell me, Raúl,
who is our creator? our Creator, Mede, is Jehovah
and then Raúl began a long, interesting, strange
discussion, about a man and a woman, the creation
of the earth, things which I had never heard
spoken about; Raúl mentioned the Bible, defined
by him as an exact book, for the first time I
heard that the Bible wasn't a despicable book;
Raúl went on to talk about his conversion; he was
a man who spent his time robbing; he was already
an expert in selecting those houses where could
practise his profession; one day he chose
a house that seemed like a good option for a
clean-out; he entered, as he was about to leave
with what he had selected he heard a noise at the
door, someone was entering, he ran and hid himself

under the bed; while he was hiding, a woman came
into the room, she took off her dress, and began
praying for the well-being of all those around
her, for the delinquents, for the needy, for all
the beings on earth; Raúl stayed rooted beneath
the bed, he felt that something inside him had
changed; how could he steal from a woman who had
just been praying for him; he waited for her to
fall asleep, he left with his hands empty; the
following day he returned to that neighbourhood,
he waited near the house until he saw the woman
leave; he followed her to her place of worship;
he listened to the words of Jehovah and from that
moment he knew that he would be a Witness; El
Chinito was released that day; Papito hurried to
occupy his bed; with the stories of the Jehovah's
Witness still echoing in my head, I made myself
available to play chess with Roberto, I beat him
three times; three weeks in captivity and for the
first time I'm sleeping like a person; it's
morning, time for roll call; the roll call ends,
I fall asleep until breakfast; in the dining room
I bump into a young guy who lives in Havana
Centre, near the Caballero de la Luz Great Masonic
Lodge in Salvador Allende Street, the old Carlos
III; the government has never touched the Lodge,
many of the regime's lawyers and doctors belong
to it; in Building Number Two, on the fourth
floor, problems, daily deaths and stabbings,
that's where the worst criminals are kept; I walk
past Orlando's cell, his voice calls me, Mede,
are you going to the courtyard today? yes,
Orlando, we'll talk there, and I left; in my cell
once more, we're grouped together, talking; I'm
surprised to hear Raúl, I'm happy here, as a

prisoner, to be able to bring the message of my
Father, Jehovah, to all of you, absolutely
everyone who is present; these words slowly sank
in, I was not expecting him to tell anyone that
he was happy in prison; it seems that no-one is
happy on the street, where all are free; happiness
lasts one second in life, it arrives and disappears
who knows where; after listening to him a lot, I
think I know why Raúl speaks like this: he's a
man who is influenced by his dreams; the days
pass, from the cell to the dining room, from the
dining room to the cell; each day is a repetition
of the day before, until it's visiting time, the
moment when we forget that waiting is becoming a
habit, the moment when we find out how things are
on the street, a time to eat better, to contemplate
the beautiful sight that the women present; it's
a time to enter paradise or to be even more alone
if your family doesn't come, if you have no
family, if your wife left you, it's a time to
want to be the prisoner who is with his family
and no-one else; they released the door; I opened
it, I went out into the corridor heading straight
for the dining room, the place where prisoners
meet when they have to go anywhere; we wait for
them to open the main door; I see a few people I
recognize, we chat, the prisoner who has the list
starts calling us according to our cards, in
alphabetical order, the names of those prisoners
who are allowed visitors; the guards do very
little work, almost all the jobs are performed by
inmates, some inmates are traitors who work for
the guards; we leave the building in lines five
deep; we arrive at the Public or Visitors' Hall;
the two story hall, the first floor for general

visits, the second, for conjugal visits that are allowed every 45 days for three or four hours; prisoners are not allowed conjugal visits for the first eight months of their sentence; an inmate's wife must bring with her a letter from her neighbourhood committee, two ID photos, her health certificate and other documents; the inmates from the women's prison, if they have a spouse in prison, may ask for conjugal rights; the Visitors' Hall is divided into three parts; the part with the cubicles where the inmates can see their lawyers; in the other two parts relations visit although they must first wait at guard post number one until they are called, but they are not called by their name, but the name of the prisoner; two or three blocks further on is the house where they check the food so that the relation doesn't try to hand over any types of drugs; although they always pass on marihuana, pills, drink; many relations traffic in drugs in the Visitors' Hall; the prisoners enter the hall before their relations do; in the hall problems always arise over seating, seats are made of cement with a long table in the middle; the first relations enter bringing with them sobs, happiness, sadness; I see Chévere's family, his wife, so distinguished, she asks me if my family knows that I'm in prison, she invites me to eat with them; I accept a glass of coffee and a cigarette from them; I stand in the entrance from where I can see the vast concentration of relations, I'm nervous, I think about my loved ones; Orlando and Dadito come up to me to chat but I don't hear them; I peer intensely, perhaps, at any moment, my family will arrive; some greet me, others pass

by, indifferent; I wait for an hour, two, maybe
they won't come now, I look again, I look into
the distance, my sister and Niurka are speaking
to the guard on duty at the entrance; my sister
goes into the cafeteria, Niurka is still speaking
to the guard; my sister returns, they keep her
there without letting her pass; Niurka comes
nearer, I wish it were my sister approaching, I
wait in the doorway, we hug each other, we kiss,
I introduce her to Orlando and to two other
prisoners I know, we sit down and immediately:
Mede, this happened to you because you don't
listen, if you had listened you wouldn't be here;
there's nothing that can be done about it now,
Niurka, if you want you can stay with me or do
whatever you wish; Papi, right now is when you
need me most, I have no intention of leaving you;
how are the girls? they're fine, it's just Yuny,
she's always asking for you, the other day the
girls were eating, Yunita pushed her plate and
spoon aside and started crying, your sister
wanted to know what the matter was; Mima, I'm
crying because I'm eating and I don't know if
Uncle Mede has food; your sister didn't say
anything to her, she went off to cry quietly; I'm
invaded by a profound nostalgia; Yuny is like the
sun and the air; always at my side, from the age
of two she slept near me, in my room, how many
times have I heard: Uncle Mede,· I love you so
much that you're like my father, not so, Daddy
Mede? Niurka tells me how she and my sister
decided to go and search for me when I didn't
arrive, one police station after another; in the
neighbourhood station, an interminable
interrogation and false information: that I'd

snuck off to the United States; that when they
knew I had arrived ok, they'd let them know; the
interrogation lasted from ten in the morning
until six in the afternoon; eventually, my sister
was exhausted, they let them go; today, they
wouldn't let Toña into the Visitors' Hall because
she hasn't got a pass with her, neither of the
two had a pass; they will be given them when they
bring a letter from the Committee, photos, ration
book, ID documents; Niurka told me about problems
that had arisen at home; she passed on hellos
from two men who lived near us, she said that she
was thinking about starting work, I agreed with
her; I gave her the receipt for the money they
took from me when I was arrested so that they
would give the money to her, I wrote a note to my
place of work so that they would pay out some
money that they owed me; she gave me the piece of
paper to collect the *jaba* that they had brought
for me; the *jaba*, a bag full of things that they
bring us, may be received by some once a month,
by others, once every two months; the roll call
starts, it is correct, they start allowing the
family members to leave, past the wardens on the
outside; the body searches begin, they have us
undress one by one; nothing can be hidden, but
something always gets through; I imagine the
homosexuals in the task of cutting a piece of
nylon, sowing it down the side, hiding in it
cigarettes, drugs, money brought by their
visitors; before going back to the cell, before
they do the body search, they go to the bathroom,
they dilate their anus with an ointment that they
get from the medicine chest on the floor where
they live, they insert the nylon tube; we leave

the Visitors' Hall, we collect what our families
have brought us or have bought for us in the
cafeteria, and we march towards our tomb; I've
cried, I've cried sometimes when the pain takes
me by surprise, or when I have no way of enduring
the repetition of a day that was exactly like the
day before; my cell mates ask after my family, I
share with them the little I could say; Lázaro,
the Jehovah's Witness, invites me to play
draughts, I don't accept, my head is driving me
crazy; in the corridor a huge dispute starts up
over some packs of cigarettes; machetes were
hauled out, they looked like two swordsmen, one
cut the other in the arm; they took the one who
had been cut to the hospital, the other, to the
punishment cell, but first, the guards gave him
a whole round of beatings; a few hours later some
inmates started drumming a beat, to sing *guaguancó*,
palo; there are several *paleros* here with their
Lucumí god, Sambiá; to become a *palero* they
perform a series of ceremonies, they sacrifice
animals, they cut the new pine, the one who is
being initiated into their religion, cutting
crosses on his chest, back, forehead; before
cutting the new pine, they bathe him with various
types of herbs, they give him *la chamba* to drink,
a mixture of gun powder, earth from the cemetery
and bones of the dead; sometimes, after drinking
la chamba he faints; the *palero* and the *santero*
do form alliances; the beat continued until a
guard arrived and ordered them to stop; the
Jehovah's Witnesses explain the importance of
life to me, that you can't live just to live, I
listen to their sermons because one should know a
little about everything, but I don't share their

beliefs; among the foreign prisoners there is
someone from Tanzania, a young boy who was
studying in Cuba, he got involved in illegal
merchandising, they never caught him for doing
business but, rather, for having four thousand
dollars in his possession, he's in prison until
the day of his court case; hearings can be delayed
for up to two years, it's all a matter of luck;
the only cases they are trying immediately are
those which have to do with Dangerousness; the
ordinary tribunals take between one day and nine
months to pass sentence; roll call is taken, I go
to bed, the days pass, all the same, Visitors'
Day rolls around for me again; we march, as
always, in line, it's cold and I have nothing to
wrap myself in; there are three women from Nuevo
Amanecer in the Visitors' Hall; the visitors
begin arriving, Chévere's relations arrived
early; I went to their table, his wife offered me
coffee, she speaks to me, Mede, La China says do
you want her to come and see you; no, because my
wife comes to see me; but so what, she can come
and see Chévere and meanwhile the two of you can
chat; ok, tell La China that she should do
whatever she wants; I chatted a little more, then
I left; families are still arriving, I wait
nervously, I wait indefinitely but they didn't
arrive; visiting hours came to an end, they count
us, they search us; I think about the pointless
waiting, I think that they have turned their
backs on me, I think that they have abandoned me,
I think that something has happened to them; they
take us to our cells; at last this sad, hard,
painful day is about to end; I huddle into a
piece of the night and cry; I have always been

able to triumph over difficulties; I know that
before success comes a time when you have to
fight, but today I don't understand these walls,
I don't understand these bars; I wanted to be
useful, I can't define myself as a delinquent,
I'm a man who has tried to survive amongst the
monsters; those who received visitors collected
the things that had been brought for them; El
Chévere came up to me, Mede, don't worry, your
sister will definitely come next Visitors' Day,
remember, she still hasn't got a visitor's pass;
another prisoner nearby wanted to upset me,
what's up, buddy, have your people sold you out?
Orlando and Dadito approached; Orlando comforts
me, don't you worry, my brother, nothing has
happened to your family, probably they weren't
allowed in; Dadito agrees, yes, I'm sure it's
like Orlando says; El Chévere comes up, take this
packet of cigarettes so that you have something
to smoke, I took the packet, opened it, shared it
with Dadito because his family is from Guantánamo
and he has no-one to bring him things, I didn't
give any to Orlando because he doesn't smoke; we
lined up in fives, as always, they took us to the
building, we entered in Indian file; in the
doorway, the official started counting us; in my
cell they ask after my family, I tell them; Bemba
immediately bursts out, oh, all women are like
that, good-for-nothings and bitches; look, Bemba,
the women you have had may have been good-for-
nothings and bitches, but not mine; we start
arguing, Papito intervenes, Bemba, you don't know
this woman so why talk like that; El Bemba gets
ready to attack, friend, you know that I'm a
bastard and I know very well what women are like;

I interfere, but not all are alike; stay out of
it, I'm not talking to you, Bemba shouts at me,
baring his teeth at me as if he were a dog; yes,
it's better that we don't talk, Bemba; drop it,
we're all brothers and we have to get on with one
another, suggests Lázaro, the Jehovah's Witness;
I'm not anyone's brother, this guy has some nerve;
Roberto interrupts, you're the one with the nerve,
Bemba, nobody spoke to you; hey, Roberto, don't
stick your nose in, nobody invited you to this
party, remember that I'm El Bemba and I don't
care if they give me another 20 years; the soldier
joins in, *caballero*, stop this argument; El Bemba
shut up immediately because he had already had a
fight with the soldier and knew that it was in
his own interest to keep quiet; at supper time,
another argument, but this time for command, for
wanting to command in the corridor; a prisoner
wants to take the command from the current
commander of the corridor, the one who is in
command of the whole wing; an argument starts
between the two; they haul out their machetes,
but no-one is harmed; their friends intervened,
as always occurs, there can't be problems between
two bullies and, when there are, they are always
sorted out; the arguments and blood-letting
generally occur in gambling, because of jealousy
between homosexual partners, over plates of food,
and for command; the prison is full of those I
call ill-fated because they cannot get used to
life on the street, they can't find direction and
return, they always return to the walls from
which they cannot learn to separate themselves;
amongst us we have Mario, the political prisoner
put in with the ordinary prisoners; Mario with

his complaints to Biqui, the young guy who was imprisoned for sabotage and who became a dental technician here in prison, and Mario is always calling him to give him an injection because he can't sleep or to bring medicine because he can't sleep and if he's not asking Biqui, then he's requesting that they take him to the doctor, that they take him to the floor's sick bay because he can't sleep; today is Mario's turn to wash his quilted blanket, I help him spread it out in the bath in the cell, upon opening it, I see all these lines of lice moving around the wet material, I stood there looking at them, I started laughing, look Mario, now you don't have to go to the doctor any more, your lack of sleep comes from your clothes; you're crazy, Mede, lice?, me?, impossible; I called my other cell mates, the lice continued to emerge from the seams, survivors of the cold water bath; *caballero*, what you have to do here is to bring the volcano and boil everyone's clothes to eliminate these bugs and their nits; we all support Papito's suggestion; they brought the two tins separated by small sticks and the two electrical cables for the plug; after boiling the clothes we saw that there was nowhere to hang them; because we're given a change of clothing every six months, we only have two changes of clothing, one for everyday wear and another for Visitors' Days; luckily, they ordered that the doors be opened so that people could go out into the courtyard to get some sun; in the courtyard I speak with two people I know; each building has its courtyard at the back, with an eight metre fence and a basketball basket; we're given courtyard privileges twice a week, for 45 minutes; today Ramón, who's about 40 years old and a prisoner for illegal possession of lard and for being a bookie, was transferred to the cell; he tells us how he arrived at his house, his wife was having a problem with the law, they had just confiscated five gallons of lard from her, and in one olive green magazine, they found a list of bets; Ramón accepted the responsibility although his wife was the one who took lard from the bakery and his wife was the bookmaker; since Ramón has been in prison, his wife has not been to see him; the prison has started a chain movement; they are emptying the penal population because the symposium will soon start and the delegations from different countries will come to tour the prisons in Havana; the political prisoners from the third floor are transferred to the fourth floor; there is chaos in Building Number Two, they are searching those prisoners who will be transferred; those on the fourth floor of Building Number 2 are, for the most part, professional assassins, the most well known of whom is Pototo the Asthmatic, who has an average of four deaths and twelve cases of having drawn blood to his name; the day after Pototo arrived from the prison in Guanajay, he killed a man and wounded two more; in Combinado there are many who have been condemned to death, cut off, awaiting their sentence; some go through three appeals, the last to the Head of State; when it is time for their execution, they take them out at dawn to the Managua military unit and there they're shot; before that, they used to have the firing squads in La Cabaña; almost all of the prisoners from the fourth floor were transferred to Kilo

Cinco y Medio in Pinar del Río; to Guanajay; to Melena Number 2 and to Quivicán in Havana; these transfers took three days, day and night; prisoners were taken from all three buildings; in Building Number 3 cells had the right number of occupants and many beds were left empty; the few prisoners who remained were issued new clothes, sheets, mattresses, towels; Combinado ended up seeming like a place for *becados,* for those who have a scholarship, not a prison; in the hospital, the same thing happened; they removed the worst cases and took them to hospitals outside; others were discharged and sent to their respective buildings; on the long awaited day, they gave us a lunch that was very good in comparison with what they usually gave us; the delegations began arriving, first they visited the military area, then they went to the factory; they entered the penal community, visiting Building Number 3, the building nearest to the entrance; then, to the hospital, where the patients waited with new pyjamas and white socks; the soldiers, who were acting as guides to the delegates, completely ignored Building Number One where the political prisoners waited to shout out their protests to the delegations; that same day they transferred us from the first to the third floor; we went through roll call called by those with the lists; we arrived on the third floor to find ourselves without sufficient beds; I thought about the box I had left in my previous cell in which I had become accustomed to keeping my few belongings, I thought about the bed I left behind while I tried to find a way to make myself comfortable on the floor; various inmates from Building Number 2

arrived to move into this same cell; I managed to
obtain a mattress which I placed between two
beds; I'm pensive and cross; I took out a notepad
to write to my dear mother, I still didn't want
her to know I was here, but today I think about
the need for her to talk to my father, fighter
from the Sierra, Head of the Ministry of the
Interior, with the rank of major; my father and
I, how little we have shared; the music plays to
signal silence, I stop writing to listen to it,
it's the sound of a music box; at roll call the
music plays followed, always, by the official's
voice: attention all prisoners, roll call is
about to commence; or, attention all prisoners,
it's time to be silent; in the next-door cell,
three prisoners armed with knives start raping a
17 year old boy; the one in charge brings a
knife to his throat: Carlitos, take off your
clothes or I'll kill you; come on, we know that
you're a *jeba*, a woman; I'm not queer, I'm a man;
cut the crap and drop your pants; another backs
him, let me stick the *enferma* with a knife and
then you'll see how quickly he gives us his butt;
Carlitos' voice can only be heard shouting: ow!
ow! and immediately, shut up, whore, if the guard
comes I'll kill you, you crazy queen; Carlitos
began sobbing while those prisoners that were
awake pretended they were sleeping; this happened
to Carlitos because they must have found out that
he is weak; I don't even know if he is a
homosexual; the convicts have categories for
homosexuals; the public, the subsistence, and
the sentimental homosexual; the public homosexual
wants the whole world to know that he is
homosexual; the subsistence homosexual offers his

services for money; the sentimental homosexual is
the one who says he was born with what he himself
calls 'this weakness' or 'this defect'; in the
day's scandal the name of some prisoner who they
have just discovered is a *jeba* is always included;
and, so-and-so is whatshisname's wife, and,
someone masturbated so that he could ejaculate on
the younger men who were sleeping and, who is
allowing himself to be seduced for food, who is
allowing himself to fall in love like a woman; in
one of the groups they spread the word that Choni
is a queer: hey, Jabico, did you know that Choni
is a queer? but, friend, that young boy looks
like a man to me, or maybe you just want to cause
him shit? no, Jabico, I swear it's true, that
he's a *jeba*, the other day, during visiting hours
a friend of mine told me; well, if you think it's
true, I'll find out because that pretty boy is
quite appetizing; the other day Carlitos didn't
go to breakfast; I know that those that raped him
didn't want him to go to the dining room so that
he couldn't tell the guards; I get to the dining
room, I start calling to my friends to find out
what section they're in; I breakfast milk and
bread; I return to my section, I lie down; some
prisoners have started to sing that sad melody of
the *guaguancós* when they speak of love; when I'm
going to leave a love, I fall in love, but today
I imagine walking towards arms that encircle a
cold smile and a taste of the tomb; the days pass
unchanging until Visitors' Day; the 9:00 a.m.
group is allowed visiting hours; the afternoon
group waits impatiently; the Head of the floor
comes up and, without explanations, announces:
attention all inmates, the visit has been

postponed until further notice; reactions varied from the pouting of a child who has had a toy taken from him to the reaction of the prisoner who is told he is to be shot; but the impulse was the same: protest; to try and get out through the dining room; the official shouted, get back to your sections or I'll call out the garrison! from the corridor we could see our families although we couldn't make them out clearly; the prisoners' uproar continued; the official charges us with a machete in his hand and his shouts: you can kill me but first I'll kill a few of you, pack of dogs; he started beating a youth of 20; two more guards arrived; us inmates run to our sections, forcing our way through to arrive quickly; the beaten youth is taken to Management accused of being the ring leader, to the punishment cell or *tapiada*, to the disciplinary section; in the disciplinary section you're only allowed to wear underclothes, and to sleep on the floor; we all closed ourselves up in our sections; the indignation was widespread, but there is no solidarity between ordinary prisoners, if we try something against the militia, one of the prisoners always gives the plan away; that same day we were transferred from the North to the South wing; when I arrived in my new section, I chose a bed on the top bunk; here El Bárbaro, a bit of a bully and a pathetic type, is in charge; here I saw the extent of the cheating and corruption; I began picking out some of the people I knew, El Chévere, Pon, Lázaro the Witness and others; Pon was imprisoned for masturbating in a public street, he's always arrested for the same thing; El Chévere and I chat about our

families; that night we ate at 9:00, a sparse and
awful meal, most times I have to fill up with
water; it's been two days since we've been in
this section and a transfer of prisoners from
Building #2, fourth floor, arrives, the ones who
came are the worst that were left, that same day
there were any number of murders and stabbings;
the people that joined my cell were all regular
prisoners, only one homosexual among them, this
character has his arms bandaged to stop him
biting his veins; whenever a homosexual can't
resolve something, they cut themselves on the
inside of their arms, parallel cuts that reach
different parts of the arm; some bullies have
seen that I'm one of the quietest people in the
section and that I'm always reading; they tried
to take my bed away from me; the head of the
section comes up to me: listen, you, I need that
bed for a friend of mine; well, *compadre*, I'm not
giving it up; I'm the one in charge here and here
you do what I say, he said to me twisting his
mouth into a strange smile; and I'm telling you
that I'm not giving you anything; well, well,
this one's gone crazy, do you know what that bit
of cheek can cost you? do what you like, I don't
care what you do; the commander began gesturing,
he made some wide movements with his hands and
called: Calluco! Calluco! bring me a machete and
let's see whether this pretty boy is tough or a
coward; in my mind's eye I saw the machete made
of metal strips heading for me, I threw myself
from the bed and grabbed a wooden stool so that
my life would cost them dearly; armed with a
towel in my left hand to ward off the blows of
the machete and the stool in my right, I saw

Calluco approach, bringing the commander a machete that looked like a samurai sword; another three prisoners approached, also with machetes; but this dance with death didn't frighten me, because we belong to it, death is the air that laps at our heels; they attacked me, the first swipe caught the bed frame, the machetes continued to rain down; I tried to dodge them as well as I could, they broke the stool with a few slashes; the towel helped me until the other inmates intervened; El Chévere managed to intercede by virtue of being a friend of the commander; the others stopped swinging their machetes; soon it was as though the whole thing had been for show, but perhaps, if I hadn't been quick enough, they would have wounded me, I'm not saying killed, because killing is a serious matter; the other inmates talked to the four prisoners armed with machetes; the head of the section called me to one side to speak to me, look, pretty boy, I know I don't have the right to take the bed away from you, but one always tries a bit of force; anyway, make sure that we don't bump heads again because nobody messes with me; I stared at him while answering: we don't have to argue about or discuss this matter, it's already in the past, but don't think that I'm scared or that you all can impress me; I watched his brow knit as he raised his voice: drop it, or I'll start thinking that you're the one who wants to frighten me; I walked away with my back towards him while thinking to myself that a roaring lion doesn't bite; I moved away with the realization that in this grave, in this hole in which they've locked us, rehabilitation is not possible; today everything

went just fine, my friends supported my behaviour;
the other day I went to the courtyard to get some
sun; I started admiring the beauty of the bit of
nature we can see, a bit of sky and the greenery
of some fields far away from the prison; they
introduce me to a man of about 45, a political
prisoner who was a guard during the Batista
regime, whom they accused of being a war criminal,
and who was condemned to 15 years; he did his
time and was set free, once free, they imprisoned
him again, falsely accusing him of having escaped,
he spent two years as a prisoner, without standing
trial, without knowing what his future would be;
when I spoke to him I found out that his father
was related to my grandfather, the famous Enrique
Despeigne, a lieutenant during the Batista
dictatorship, shot during the Revolution's
successful completion; I began feeling a deep
compassion for this man but refrained from
showing it; in this place there is no room for
demonstrations or expressions of emotion; through
him I became friendly with several political
prisoners; most of the political prisoners have
been prisoners for 21 years; that same day I made
my way through to the floor where the *plantados*
stay; prisoners are re-educated in prison, but
some political prisoners reject the whole system
of re-education and these are called *plantados*;
they are identifiable because they wear white
shorts made from sheets; the other political
prisoners wear yellow; *plantados* are not released
even when they have served out their sentence; I
felt comfortable amongst them; the presence of
these long-suffering men was a balm; I went on to
the wing where the foreign prisoners stay; I

spent many long hours talking to them; when I left they gave me American newspapers and magazines; one of them gave me a box of Morris cigarettes; I already knew all the North American prisoners from Guanajay prison; I was there one sad day when they rebelled and two were killed; others were beaten; one tall, thin prisoner had his eye taken out; I thought that it is sad to come from another land and be humiliated; I thought that while one knows where one is born, one doesn't know where one will find suffering; the guards ask us which of us had our Visitors' Day postponed so that we can fill out telegrams advising our relations of the date of the next Visitors' Day; at the moment I'm seated in the dining room, and next to me sits a man of about 35 years, of average build; I'm absorbed in the task of eating, suddenly, a river of blood appears on my tray, it stains my shirt, I realised then that the man next to me had been stabbed; the problem had to do with a homosexual who lived with the attacker and who had been taken away from him by the victim; with the first blows the man fell to the floor, I witnessed his life leaving him; the killer stopped with the bloody knife in his hand and shouted: who is the next *enferma* who wants to die like this one did? and began kicking the body; finally a guard arrived, took the knife from him, and took him to Management; I remained calm until the assassin disappeared; when he was out of sight, I knelt beside the victim to see if he was alive; I took his pulse, although his skin was still warm, I could feel nothing, I lifted his shirt to see if his heart was still beating; it was still; with one of the blows to his back, the knife had gone straight through his heart; that was why I hadn't even heard him cry out when the jet of blood had landed on me; I walk away from the dining room thinking that this place is a kind of purgatory; the victim as a topic of conversation even spread to the streets of Havana; the awaited day arrives, it's Visitors' Day, it will be a sad day for me; in the Visitors' Hall there are a number of fights, all unimportant; relatives tell us that on the day that Visitors' Day was cancelled they all protested but to no avail; they were threatened that, if they didn't leave, the garrison would be called out, mothers with children in their arms, old women, pregnant women, all asked for the same thing, that they be given news of their imprisoned relations, but all information was denied them; the visitors left with the food they had brought for the inmates, obtained with such difficulty; they treat the relations that come to see us as if they are dogs, when visiting time is over and it's raining, they chase them out without caring whether children and old people get wet; Chévere's sister came, she talks to me, Mede, if you promise to come back to me, I will always come and visit you; China, I'm not trying to deceive you, I need someone to come and visit me but I can't promise you something that I don't feel for you, to me you are only a very good acquaintance, I can't call you my friend, because friends don't feel what you feel for me; look, Mede, save that for someone else, the trouble with you is that you still feel something for that woman; it's true that I still love her, I'll stop loving her when

I know the truth about all this; it's always the same, Mede, you love them when they don't love you, but be aware of the critical situation that you're in, you need a woman who loves you and I could be that woman; she kissed me in a passionate, sensual embrace; I think that loving the woman who left me is a matter of destiny, I still care for Niurka, why deny it; La China lets me go, she talks to me about the situation in the street, that there have been acts of sabotage, that wherever you look there are protest posters; I imagine myself making a clandestine contribution, involved in the turmoil in the streets, but the visit ends and I carry with me the painful wait for my loved ones; back in my section, the same diet of annoyances, gambling, drug taking and loan sharks collecting their debts; there are cigarette loan sharks who will give you five cigarettes on the understanding that you give them back a full packet and if you don't pay them, then it's time to stab and kill for a few cigarettes or for a few pesos; the addicts are always looking for something to give them a high or get them drunk; when they can't find anything they'll even drink perfume; El Sublime ingests anti-asthmatic bottles, gets a high and starts singing *guaguancó*; another who was always drunk was Santos Ortega, an older man, he pretended to have asthma attacks so that they would give him anti-asthmatics; sometimes they ignored him, one day they took him to the pharmacy area, they gave him three bottles which he gulped down, after finishing the three bottles he started shouting that he was dying, that he didn't want his daughter orphaned, that they should save him;

they came to fetch him, he died before reaching
the hospital; when they told me the only thing I
remembered about Santos was that he hardly ever
ate and that his daily occupation was to find
something to get drunk on; I've realised that any
day now there's going to be big shit between the
boy in the next cell and a man that's in my group,
the boy is about 20 years old, he's from the
Jesús María neighbourhood; everyone knows that
the man cut the face of the boy's mother and we
know that something's going to happen; the guards
start taking roll call; the head of the section
gives the order to stand at attention, the order
to go to breakfast; we head for the dining room;
suddenly, the boy comes like a lightening flash
out of an empty hall and stabs the man in his
right lung, the man takes off, shouting, but the
boy follows him; now in the dining room he stabs
him again in his arm; the man continues trying to
get away now almost on all fours; the boy stabs
him again but the blows land in air; the inmates
protect themselves leaning against the wall; the
uproar is general; we hear the shouts, *caballero*,
stop that one who's trying to kill me, for God's
sake, help me, I don't want to die! three inmates
climbed up the boy to try and take the bayonet
away from him; two guards appear and one of them
shouts at the boy, drop that, you've already done
him enough damage; the now unconscious man,
streaming blood, is taken to hospital; the boy is
taken to Management; already the letting of blood
with drawn machetes is a habit and the news of
the day, hey, buddy, did you hear? so-and-so was
stabbed; one morning they took my group out of
our cell, the building was full of guards, they

started to inspect us one by one; they sent us
down to the courtyard in Indian file; before
going, we were ordered to remove our clothes,
even our underwear; they pushed us down the
stairs; we reached the courtyard which was
surrounded by escorts on the outside; two escorts
aimed teargas rifles at us; they seated us in
rows according to our floor and wing; the
inspections continued: cells, sections, dining
rooms, floors; the day advances and we remain in
the courtyard without eating, without drinking
any water; at about two in the afternoon, a heavy
rain chills us, we have nothing to cover ourselves
with, some of us get together to give the guards
a hard time, but their weapons rain down on us,
we feel the blows fall on our backs, on our
bodies; we start scattering; two fall down
wounded, the blows cease at the voice of the
Chief of the Penal Re-educators; the Chief of
Security joins the other guards; the old men
start disappearing towards their cells; the
cripples; at last it is our turn to go back; we
arrive at our section, all our belongings are
strewn around the floor; the corridor, full of
clothes, shoes thrown down; we take stock, things
are missing, without any explanation, the voices
of the guards: what's missing has been confiscated;
they could have said: it's been stolen, because
that's the practise, to steal from us the things
that they take a fancy to; usually the object of
these inspections is to search for sharp
instruments that may be used as weapons, anything
with a cutting edge; but these searches are not
thorough: we've just heard the news about two
people wounded on the second floor; that same day

a chain from La Cabaña Prison arrived and
departed; amongst those in the chain was an enemy
of Pomares, someone who had stabbed him in the
stomach; when I see Pomares that day in charge of
dishing out food I am a little surprised but I
don't pay much attention; they release the North
wing so that the prisoners can come and eat;
Pomares joins the group and starts stabbing the
man; his enemy falls to the floor, he lived
because people intervened; the official on duty
takes Pomares, the other man disappears to the
hospital; my relationship with the political
prisoners strengthens; the commander of the
corridor on that floor is an acquaintance of
mine, I can stay out, I climb one side of the
building until I reach the fourth floor; it's a
pleasure to share ideals, it's a pleasure to know
that here machete duels are non-existent; here
are the ones who write poetry, those devoted to
reading, the ones who make rings and chains, the
weavers of panties, bras, pullovers, blankets; a
few days ago Juan Sin Miedo arrived in the cell
next door, he's a big bully who was in hospital
after being stabbed, today he was taken back
after being stabbed in his hand; still in the
cell is El Manía, who is also a bully, but only
with youngsters who have little experience in
prison ways, with us, he always keeps quiet; most
prison friendships are formed as the result of
the *jaba*; whenever someone's relations bring him
a bag of food, prisoners gather round, afterwards
they disappear with what they've managed to take
from him; whenever some presentable young guy
arrives there is always a bully who shouts:
caballero, I don't want anyone messing with this

guy, his father is like my brother; but we know
that the bully doesn't know the young guy's father
although he repeats: listen, nephew, did you know
that your father is a friend of mine? more than
that, your father is like a brother to me; listen,
nephew, you have my bed, I'll sleep on the floor;
and that night the fun starts, hey, pretty boy, I
can't get to sleep, the floor's as hard as a
rock, why don't you give me a bit of the bed?
we're going to have to call Ramón "Ramón the
Suicide", he's always trying to kill himself, the
other day he tried to swallow some blades, he
couldn't because the other prisoners intervened;
that same day he tried to hang himself at lunch
time; this place if full of people on the verge
of a nervous breakdown who receive no treatment
of any sort; today is Valentine's Day, I write a
letter to Niurka, a postcard that I made, I write
two letters to my sister, I took them out on
Visitors' Day; in my section, I form a new
friendship, Chon, who is like a brother to me,
the same as Machacho; during Visiting Hours they
inform me that the country is still in turmoil;
they tell me about Captain David who speaks to
the people from a radio station, some say he'll
be our leader, no-one knows who he is; propaganda
against the government increases in the streets;
a horse walks through the streets of Havana
bearing the sign: son, look what you've done to
me; the prisons are packed; they transfer me to
another wing on the same floor; yet again I have
to sleep on the floor; Chon and I plan an escape
through the main door of the building; when we
get to the roof garden, Chon chickens out, he
refuses, we return to our cell and I think about

the freedom being enjoyed by the two prisoners
who escaped last week, one dressed as a woman,
the other dressed in military uniform; through
Chon's mother I find out about the secret exodus
to the U.S.A., and I regret not being in the
street, involved in sabotage, on death's edge;
here instead, with a quick mind and a body that
moves at slow, repeated paces; an uprising takes
place in the cell for minors, they overturned the
beds and put them in the corridor so that the
guards couldn't get past; the floor commander
came and tried to get through, the minors threw
medicine bottles at him; the minors want the
adults to join the uprising, nobody even moved;
they ask the political prisoners for protection,
the garrison arrives, armed to the teeth; the
political prisoners protest, they threaten a
revolt if the minors are touched; the Chief of
Security decides to placate the rioters without
using violence, the head of the floor was sent
for punishment to the cordon guards; Pirulí, the
corridor commander had an argument with his
friend Izquierdo; the friend pulled a knife on
him, Pirulí snatched it from him and started
stabbing him; Izquierdo was taken in a critical
state to an outside hospital; Pirulí ended up in
the punishment cell with a cut hand but a few
days later was back and up to his bullying again;
they say that some inmates bribed the *tapiada*
guard to release Pirulí; here at the moment there
are some *ñáñigos* or *abacuás*, members of a secret
society, with their exaggerated and strange
concept of manliness; there are various branches
or houses of *ñáñigos*: *abacuá en fo*; *enduré*, *orú*,
entá, *orí*, *bibí*, *gumán*, *canfioró*, *camaroró*; in

the national folk dancing the *abacuá* has a dance in which the *ñáñigo* appears dressed as a devil, the *Ilimo*, with horns and a tail, dressed in sack cloth; they start dancing, holding a rod; in the prisons, a *ñáñigo* is more respected than any other man: an *abacuá* always finds a bed available when he arrives; he always has more than enough food; several men that were transferred from Building #3 joined our section, among them, an ex-Emigration lieutenant, about 33 years old, of average build; he graduated from the Ministry of the Interior, he had a yacht, he was thinking about leaving the country illegally; he was denounced to State Security; we receive news about an attack on the Peruvian Embassy, of the removal of the guards who were outside the Embassy, of the political asylum in the Embassy; Building #3 is emptied to receive those taken prisoner during Operation Inca, those that were detained for being in the vicinity of the Embassy; the director of the prison decided to create an urgent chain, many inmates were transferred to other prisons; the guards don't allow Operation Inca prisoners to sleep, they're beaten, treated like dogs; we knew that ten thousand people had found asylum in the Embassy, I was dying to be out on the street, to seek asylum, I don't know what to do; but, Mede, my brother, are you crazy? to escape at this time is to commit suicide; it's even crazier to stay in this filthy place, Orlando; but don't you understand, Mede, that our time is coming? how can it be coming if those boats are only going to take relations? because these people, at the first opportunity that presents itself, will get rid of us, you'll see;

I started thinking that Orlando was right, I
calmed down; but news keeps coming, boats,
launches, and yachts, have started to arrive from
Cayo Hueso, it's two in the afternoon, it's
raining, I'm in front of the television, I go and
find my section, I take a change of home-made
clothes out of my mattress, I dress, Orlando
stops me: Mede, what are you doing with those
clothes? I know that Orlando is right, I give up
the idea of escaping; days pass in waiting; news
of a woman run over by a car in a demonstration;
the driver of the car was killed by guards; people
from Operation Inca start disappearing from
Building #3, we knew that they were being sent to
the U.S.A.; that night they give us the forms;
between enjoyment and happiness we fear a
practical joke; the next day they call me to sign
up, what do you think about the government? I
told them what I thought; they ordered me to
depart without signing me up; news of ex political
prisoners with asylum in the Office of U.S.
Affairs; the workers and the students, in a pre-
planned attack, assault the ex-prisoners;
Visitors' Day arrived with all its great drama; I
wait for a visit from my loved ones, but only La
China arrives, we kiss in an embrace, I felt in
myself a need for her kiss; we speak about the
street, about our private life, I thought she
would try and hold me back, but she says, Mede,
it's better that you go to the U.S.A., for the
good of both of us; if you promise to stay with
me, I'll go with you; *mi vida*, I intend going,
but I can't promise you anything; Papi, you're
mean to me, I'd rather resign myself to not
having you than having to listen to these rebukes;

I didn't want to continue with the conversation,
I left to speak to Chon's mother, my mother, what
are things like outside in the street? son, things
are bad, they came to my house for my other son,
said that if he didn't go, they would give him
four years for Dangerousness; I try to console
her, I feel myself crying with her, sobs that
don't show; six months without seeing my loved
ones, and now, will life with its surprises take
me far from them forever without them even
knowing it? happiness, definitely, comes to us
seldom, for a tiny fraction of time; Chévere's
wife speaks about her plans to seek asylum in the
Embassy with her children; El Chévere talks about
his departure for the U.S.A.; Chévere's mother
has given her approval; from last night the
prisoners have started leaving Building #1,
perhaps they leave with the happiness of the
free, perhaps with apprehension about the unknown;
some mothers, upon arriving at the Visitors' Hall
and not seeing their sons, suffer attacks, they
are taken to hospital; the list of those who are
to leave arrives; tears, goodbyes; the visitors
leave down the path that leads to the countryside
that is so loved by all of us; I hugged those
that on my sad days gave peace to my soul; I look
back in time to hug my loved ones; La China comes
up to me, she cries on my shoulder, during our
embrace, Mede, one day, if you want a true love,
look for me; write when you get there; she moves
away from me, runs towards the door, she
disappears; in my section a drawn out aloneness
awaits; in the narrowness of my bed time contracts,
Yuny, Yardely, I can almost touch them; during
the night four Girones buses carry us away from

our loved ones; a chain from La Cabaña Prison
comes in, these are prisoners who had rejected
leaving the country because of their families; La
Cabaña ended up as a distribution centre for
those that arrived from prisons in the country's
interior and from where they will be sent to
Mariel; the first prisoners they took out of
prison were those with the longest sentences, the
professional assassins, the abnormal ones, the
dregs; I remembered Orlando's words, about what
they were going to do with us; day after day we
concentrated on the one who informed us about the
boats that arrived and departed; he became the
centre of attention; rivalries for power in the
dining room and for command decreased; plans were
made for a future in the United States: when I
arrive in *Yuma* I'm going to join the Mafia; or, I
have to kill so-and-so, I'll catch him in *Yuma*;
some made honest plans; El Chévere's turn to
leave arrived, seeing him leave I felt alone, a
good man, El Chévere; guards arrive with a card
that indicates my departure; I leave Machacho
getting ready to leave too; Orlando's cell, we
say our goodbyes; one of the guards shouts at us,
bunch of traitors, I hope you come back like
those from Girón Beach returned so that we can do
the same to you! they put us on the second floor
in Building #3; we had no sheets, but, for the
first time, no-one had to sleep on the floor; the
insult about traitors was made ridiculous by the
guards' contradictions: you're all scum, that's
why society has decided to export you to the
United States; we applauded as if that were a
victory for us; remaining behind were the
political prisoners, the *lancheros*; day breaks,

time for roll call arrives with the ill treatment of the guards who, deep down, resent being excluded from the exodus to Mariel; while I wait for our departure, I turn 23, I imagine celebrating my birthday away from here; we feel wretched, our anguish increases when we hear the news that Carter doesn't want any more Cubans and he wants the empty boats to return to Cayo Hueso; departures from Combinado have been discontinued; no buses arrive, only more prisoners from around the country; we have no cigarettes, the food is worse than ever; one of the 27 prisoners in my cell offers me a *tupamaro* made from mattress stuffing; on other occasions we smoke *brevas* made from threads from our own clothes; one of the guards got carried away with his image of himself as a karate expert, carrying with him his **oquendo** sticks; today, apart from irritating us with his sticks, he throws water at us carried in serum bottles, he insults us; it's our turn for a Visitors' Day but we're not allowed to go to the Hall; from far off I see La China, I call her at the top of my voice, she doesn't hear me; her persistence hurt me a little, her habit of refusing to accept my lack of attention, of not seeing that the birds have flown and the flowers stop blooming; China, I want to make you real one more time, and now you can't hear me; it's been more than 24 hours since we have ingested anything, we protest, beating the bars; the inmates from other sections follow our lead; the garrison arrives, we see rods and machetes descending; we feel the pain of the blows on our faces, of the closed fists; they throw El Colorado to the floor, a guard stands on him, starts

jumping; the beating ceases, we enter our cell;
they take three critically injured prisoners
away; a few days pass, they arrive with a list,
they transfer us to another wing; in the new
cell, another new list, they line us up in Indian
file; I drop my towel, my soap, into a box; on
the first floor they take our prison clothes,
they give us civilian clothes, the same ones they
had taken from us when we entered the penitentiary,
the shoes were new, we call them 'we all have
them' because they're all identical and all the
same colour; an inmate comes up to me, *paisano*,
now we're definitely going, when I get there, I'm
going to take off this shit and I'm going to wear
Yuma clothes, because there, as you already know,
nobody wants for anything; some inmates smoke,
others collect cigarette butts to make *brevas*; a
guard shouts at us, hey! you're smoking like
presidents; but *combatiente*, don't you smoke?
that's none of your business; but *combatiente*,
that's not nice; I'll answer however I like; I
realised that it would be best for me to move
away from this guard who was so determined to
show off; they moved us up to a cell full of
couples, each active homosexual with his passive
partner, originally from Building #2; the whole
night is full of the noise of buses that take a
chain from the other buildings to penitentiary
centres where the transferred prisoners are to
work, most of the country's production is produced
by prisoners; the day dawned with that beautiful
brilliance that a Cuban morning has, in the sky,
so intense, birds circle; several buses arrive,
they take us down to the first floor; the
loudspeaker shouts at us, up against the wall,

let's see, you, move over there, hurry up, pack
of! I thought to myself that they were offending
us for the last time; they ordered me to get into
the bus, hey, scum, are you going to the United
States so that they can throw you to the dogs?
that will be better than to live like a dog, I
dared reply; in the bus, two escorts, three
prisoners in each seat; we form a convoy of eight
buses; they pulled us from the tomb, we're on our
way; I'm nervous, I am aware of my body trembling,
it's difficult for me to keep back my tears, I
think about my loved ones; will this absence of
six months and twenty one days become forever?
cars that come across us recognise that we are
from prison, we are accompanied by three cars
from Emigration, they can see into the buses, see
the escorts; I seem to feel the contempt of those
that pass by; I look at the Ocho Vías scenery;
the sun is becoming too ruddy, as happens in the
month of May; the trees accompany us, we cross
the Ocho Vías bridge that goes to Guanabacoa; the
patrol car follows us; in the distance one can
see Alamar with its modern constructions; the
green of the cattle farms; don't open the window,
you wretch, can't you hear? anyone who's feeling
brave can try, I'll break his head with my KM;
we're completely enclosed in an interprovincial
bus that is unbearably hot; we leave Eastern
Havana behind; we are approaching the tunnel;
the entrance to the bay, the sea so blue out of
the window; upon entering the tunnel the buses
pull closer together; I look at the Prado, so
beautiful, I see myself walking through it as I
have done so many times; we enter the Malecón,
the voices from the street define us as scum with

their shouts; reaching El Vedado, I feel the
proximity of my house; the Miramar Tunnel, my
house nearby, there's no way to say goodbye; all
I can feel are the wheels turning; the Miramar
residential area is chaotic; the militia looking
for their prey like dogs; convoys of cars through
the Quinta Avenida; there are at least four blocks
full of guards around the Peruvian Embassy,
guarding it; the streets have been totally taken
over by the military; a few straggling civilians
say goodbye to us; I tried to get up from my seat,
the guard's shout stopped me, filth, traitor,
don't you know you can't get out of your seat?
the traitors are the ones who have enslaved the
people since 59; I see the butt of his rifle
coming towards me to smash me but the sergeant
stops him; leave him, he'll learn his lesson when
he's with the Yankees; I recall José Martí's
face, truth exists to be told, not to be hidden;
Martí, don't let tyrants hide their faces behind
masks woven from your words; is it too late to
rejoin the struggle? is it too late for your
second death hidden in the Dos Ríos brushland?
we've been out of hell for 45 minutes, we sense
the entrance to Mosquito; we find several
different sections, for relations, for prisoners
from Nuevo Amanecer and other prisons for women;
there is a section for single men from the street;
another for prisoners from around the country;
the sea's beauty reaches us; on a small, rocky
hill you can see guards with 30 calibre machine
guns and some with KMs surveying those leaving; I
see a house with radar; the buses stop; the
prisoners have their names called out; the buses
empty, they line us up in groups five wide and

five deep, a captain gives us a lecture like so
many others we have heard before: prison
population, today our Commander in Chief is
giving you the opportunity to leave the country,
for this reason I'm reminding you that from the
exact moment that you board the vessel assigned
to you, you cease to be prisoners, you owe nothing
to society, except that, if any of you regret
having left the country and wish to return, you
will be placed back in prison; those of you
leaving today must deny in the United States that
you have come from prison; you must assert that
you were given asylum by the Peruvian Embassy; if
you do not do this you will be imprisoned in the
United States; the captain repeated the same
thing to us several times until he left;
afterwards we were called up according to a list
to be given a piece of paper we were not to lose
as we were to hand it in when we caught the bus
that would take us to Mariel, they would give us
another that we would have to hand in when we
boarded our vessels; the whole area had a cordon
of guards who set their German Shepherds on to us
and who harassed us with shouts of scum, scum;
there were four tents all full of prisoners; many
of them on wooden beds, others on mattresses
thrown on boards; Orlando and I found each other,
we hugged; they shout my sister's name over the
loud-speaker using her mother's surname; I
approach Orlando, listen, they said my sister's
name; yes, Mede, but God alone knows if it's her;
I can't stay here, without knowing, I run through
the cordon of guards, I reach the section where
the relations are; there is a complete lack of
hygiene, the odour of urine, of excrement, is

unbearable; I don't have time to verify anything; a guard falls on me from behind, he grabs me by the collar of my shirt; he shouts a few swearwords at me; he takes me to the official on duty, I hear him shout at me: give me the piece of paper we gave you, you're going back to Combinado right now; I didn't know we weren't allowed in here, forgive me, *combatiente*; that's right, beg forgiveness like a sissy; several voices are heard arguing about my punishment, what this one needs is a round of beatings so that he learns respect; leave him, I'm the one who's going to sort him out, said a guard I know from Combinado; the other guards return to their posts, do you want to learn a little respect for the guards before leaving? what did you do that for? all of you are a bunch of idiots, why don't you answer so that I can knock your teeth in? I kept quiet until I heard him insulting my mother, I was about to reply, he interrupted me: you're safe because you're a wretch and I remember you from Combinado, because if it weren't so, I'd beat you to death; thank you very much, *combatiente*, I promise I won't do it again; alright, get going, get out of my sight before I give you a kick; he held out the piece of paper to me which I took quickly; permission to withdraw, *combatiente*; go to hell, I heard him say while moving off; I returned to my companions, it was three in the afternoon, the 25th, May, Sunday, 1980; our drinking water came from the dirty tanks where it had been deposited; the sea, a few steps away, looked choppy; in the distance, the yachts, boats, and launches the Cubans from the Community had brought to fetch their relations; the civilians were near us, we were separated from them by a rope and a cordon of guards; they were worse off than we were; they had to sleep on the bare ground or on the rocks at the sea's edge; there was one tent for all of them but they couldn't all fit; the civilians' bathrooms were like pigsties; they all carried their passports and their safe conduct passes so that the Americans would believe that they had come from the Peruvian Embassy; passports were issued to civilians at the Cuatro Ruedas Police Station, they had to wait there for several days before being transferred to Mosquito; at Cuatro Ruedas they had to pay for everything they ate; women, children, men were all housed together, they had no baths in which to wash themselves; at Mosquito they gave us yoghurt for breakfast; for lunch, always a sparse, sour, repetitive meal, we had white rice with processed meat; there is a coming and going of cars that take the deportees to Mariel; a small launch bearing the American flag approaches, the guard aims his KM at it, the launch returns to the open sea, the guard lowers his weapon; at lunch time the families came out to eat in Indian file; the guards pushed them, treated them disgracefully, I had never seen so much abuse, so much shoving about of women, old people and children; the prisoners are shifted more quickly, the government is in a hurry to rid itself of the assassins; about twenty metres from the tents where us prisoners are, there is a tent for the drivers who take us to Mariel; the prisoners carefully sift through the soil for cigarette butts to make *brevas* with; I haven't smoked for more than 72 hours; amongst us, there

were some prisoners who had their passports and
safe conduct passes from the Peruvian Embassy,
even though they didn't have a clue where the
Embassy was; the muddy ground makes sleeping
difficult for those who have to sleep on it; one
of the guards sets his dog on a prisoner who
tried to talk to a civilian, the dog destroyed
his trousers, bit him in the leg, while the youth
falls about screaming, the guard smiles as if he
were watching a beautiful sight, I wanted to
shout at him, executioner, butterfly killer, but
I kept quiet; during this hiatus, some of those
who were enemies in prison established a temporary
friendship; Mosquito was like an anthill; the
loudspeakers started shouting, family members of
vessel number 5698 called Marilyn please go to
point number 2, ready to board; the Cuban music
was interrupted every now and then with departure
announcements; I rest for a bit, I try to relax
within a mixture of happiness and nostalgia which
gives way to an indifference which stretches into
infinity; I ask myself where I will die and am
seized by an urgent need to have my remains
returned to Cuban soil; I'm in the bus which is
taking me to Mariel; on the seat I leave my sworn
promise to return; it's two in the morning, the
road is lined with guards; the seats, replete
with ex-prisoners, I start to hum a sad song to
leave it lighting up the night; we pass the Power
Station, the cement factory; we are approaching
the port; a guard does a head count, makes a note
of the exact number of prisoners; we can see
several tuna fishing boats in the process of
being repaired; movement ceases, we get off the
bus in Indian file; the lights from the vessels

allow us to make out the sea transformed into an
enormous, floating city; we can hear American
music; on one side you can see the relations that
have come to collect their family members; they
seemed to be partying in those kiosks where even
water is sold at an exorbitant price; they put us
in a warehouse where others were already awaiting
their departure; the warehouse, large and wide,
the door guarded by two officials from the
Ministry of the Interior; around the warehouse
there is much movement of soldiers; periodically
we heard the call going out to the vessels that
were to approach the wharves; our group is made
up almost entirely of prisoners; one woman
addresses the official, lieutenant, my brother
has come to fetch me in a shrimp trawler, if you
call him, we can get almost everyone here on
board; wait, I'll call the coast guard and find
out if they accept; we watched him move away from
us; the woman talks to us, brothers and sisters,
let's see if we can all go together; the woman is
about 30 years old, short, very fair, her blonde
hair down to her shoulders; in the group we start
conversing but are interrupted by the guard's
shout: silence! I need to go, please may I,
combatiente, please let me go to the toilet? yes,
you can go, but don't take too long; I left the
warehouse that, to me, felt like a fridge, I
began enjoying the morning which still held a
starry sky, a silvery moon; I feel as though I'm
joined in an almost goodbye uttered in silence; I
began collecting images, back to back; on the
wharf, several vessels waiting; the bathrooms,
divided, for gentlemen, for ladies; in the
distance, the military unit from La Marina de

Guerra; I often visited that unit to see Papito,
who worked in a flotilla of torpedo launches;
Papito committed suicide by shooting himself in
the heart, because of family problems; upon my
return to the warehouse, Chicho la Ritmo, the
guaguancó singer, is speaking to the official: I
don't believe in any of you and I'm not going to
be intimidated by you, even if you refuse to let
me leave; let's see how brave you are when I take
you to the little room; what, are you and your
gang going to beat me up? no, I'm going to beat
you up by myself; an agitated voice tries to stop
the argument, drop it, Chicho, please, drop it;
it was the voice of a young boy, Chicho's wife in
the prison's building for homosexuals; sit down
and don't get involved in this, nothing's going
to happen to me; the guard disappears into a
room, followed by Chicho; the boy, now desperate,
obsessively repeats, if Chicho isn't allowed to
go, I'm not going either; another homosexual
comments, referring to the boy, I don't know why
Moraima puts up with Chicho; Moraima defends his
position, there's nothing to put up with, Chicho
is the man of my life and where he goes I go; the
homosexuals coupled up in prison, those that
called themselves women plucked their eyebrows;
the official arrived, madam, your brother's
vessel is docked at the wharf, you should go and
speak to him; the woman left the warehouse behind
the official; Chicho la Ritmo returned with the
soldier in a cordial mood; strangely enough it
seems that they had sorted things out; Moraima
went up to Chicho and took him by the arm to sit
down away from everyone else; again I'm invaded
by a need to run out into the street, to cross

the city, to embrace those I love; I try to
distract myself, I start chatting to a man who is
from outside, brother, do you have family in the
United States? are you speaking to me? yes, I
answered; well, yes, I have three brothers that
left at the start of the Revolution; are they
coming to fetch you? no, I had to go through a
lot just to be here, look, this is my family; he
pointed several people seated on a bench out to
me, a thin, older woman with grey hair; a slim
girl of about 26 with a child in her arms; three
men who looked like her brothers; and where are
you from? given my unkempt appearance I didn't
have to explain too much; I'm from prison, from
Combinado del Este Prison; when all is said and
done you prisoners can't complain, it has been
easy for you to solve the problem of leaving the
country, unlike my family and I, for us it was
very difficult, I went to the Police Station to
organise my departure but they didn't want to let
me leave because I didn't have a criminal record,
I had to tell them that I was a homosexual and
that my lover was my daughter's husband; the man
pointed out a young man seated next to his
daughter, he continued speaking; I put my two
sons down as passive homosexuals; when the guard
asked me if no-one in my house liked women, I
said yes, that both my wife and daughter did; I
started laughing, and the man found my laughter
contagious; after negotiating my departure, the
most painful part was facing my neighbours from
our block and hearing the shouts of scum, scum,
you're going to *El Norte* to sell yourself for
American jeans, sometimes this shame was
accompanied by a shower of rotten eggs, tomatoes;

many of those that were leaving too also took
part in this despicable action; we went out in
groups of 20 to the boat; the voice of the
official could be heard, that group, join the
queue, faster, walk faster; hey you, don't try
and sneak in, wait your turn; when I reached the
shrimp trawler, another official gave instructions,
the boat had too many people on board, we nearly
didn't fit; nearby, another boat was loading
people; ours was so full that there were even
people on the roof; the boat's officer protested,
but the guard insisted, I've been ordered to put
them on this boat; once his orders had been
carried out, he left; the one in charge of the
boat speaks to us, brothers and sisters, you are
now free, you are now protected by the American
flag; I thought about the slaves from long ago, I
felt like a modern slave breaking my chains in a
shrimp trawler that consisted of a cabin, a hold,
an engine room, the helmsman's cabin; as we
pulled away I saw the guard who had organised our
departure trying to contain his tears; in the
stern, a tarpaulin protected us from the sun and
there were some benches where the women, children
and old people sat; an elderly woman comes up to
me, son, would you like some coffee and a seasick
pill? yes, mother, that would be great; I watched
her move off towards the cabin; I looked back,
towards the port, and I felt myself crying; it
seemed to me that the only thing that existed was
the noise of the waves crashing in my silence; we
stopped in the bay to wait for the flotilla of
vessels; in the distance, the lights of the
community of Mariel; the sun starts to show on
the horizon to give us a beautiful dawn, the

vessels hurry, heading North; we move away from
the coast, only destiny knows what it has in
store for us; a woman vomits, retches, they take
her to the cabin, she appears later, a little
calmer; they offer us coffee, sodas, cigarettes;
the cigarette that they gave me had a bitter
taste, I'm not used these American cigarettes;
next to me, two young people talk to each other,
life's like that, I already feel like an American;
yes, my friend, that's all very well so long as
this tub doesn't tip over; and why should it tip
over? stop being such a drama queen, buddy, I'm
not in the mood for disaster stories; the boat's
helmsman is a 70 year old North American, black,
with fluid movements, missing his left eye; the
man who had come to fetch his sister was about 35
years old, as fat as a barrel of lard, with fair
skin, burnt by the sun; the seagulls looked like
guardians from space behind our boat; the flying
fish played in the waves; there is no other vessel
near us, just the sea to keep us company, and the
infinite sky; I can't find a spot to sleep, to
give my sadness a rest; I haven't slept for more
than 48 hours; at about 11:00 in the morning they
give us a small ham sandwich and a glass of soda;
three of the people who came from prison head for
the cabin to steal food; I reprimanded them; they
insulted me, what we do is none of your business,
or maybe you're a sneak? no, I'm no sneak, but if
you do that here, I can imagine what you would do
in the street; fine, you've won for today, but
wait until we catch you on the street; we can
meet wherever you like, I said; I saw his mouth
open, trying to insult me, but the noise of the
engine hampered him; the sun brings with it a

suffocating heat; while I do think that life at
sea must be beautiful, I feel a need to be on dry
land, this solitary beauty makes you too sad; an
American helicopter flies by us, it takes a
number of photos; several people are ill, they
bring them alcohol to alleviate their nausea; I
see a shark from close up, so many strange fish;
two men are talking near me, do you know that I
always dreamt about this escape? for my part I
never thought about leaving Cuba, but the
situation deteriorates daily; they continued
talking until a wave washed over all of us who
were sitting near the prow; a man broke into
screams, I don't want to die, I don't want to
die! in truth it was frightening, the way the
boat rose and fell, stopping sometimes because
the motor failed, so much so that it seemed about
to sink; it began to rain torrentially, we had
nowhere to take refuge; we all thought that we
were going to be shipwrecked; the man captaining
the boat tried to calm us down: brothers and
sisters, don't be afraid, I promise you that
nothing will happen, this small storm will pass
from one moment to the next; soon we'll all have
arrived safely; while he was talking I thought
that most probably he was more frightened than
the rest of us; the motors kept cutting out; the
older man left the helmsman's cabin and went to
the engine room; he came up again; he spoke to a
young sailor in words that I didn't understand;
the young man translated for us in perfect
Spanish: try to spread yourselves throughout the
boat, if you all sit in the same place, we might
sink; immediately thereafter he started fetching
life jackets from the hold and sharing them out

amongst us; I realised then just how serious the
situation was, I sat myself on the deck of the
boat to await my end; I rested my head against
the cabin wall of the shrimp trawler, closed my
eyes, and fell asleep; when I awoke, the storm
was over, and the afternoon was fading to give
way to night; the stars started coming out, the
sea became as dark as a tomb; some voices
accelerate the beat of my heart: look, look there,
you can see some lights, we're arriving! I quickly
searched in the distance for the lights like
fireflies; several buoys, there are rocks sticking
out; the boat heads for the entrance, we've
reached Cayo Hueso; I felt happy to be approaching
this country having refused to believe Cuban
propaganda about it: in the U.S.A. blacks are
thrown to the dogs; the swell had dropped; a
coastguard launch approached the boat; one of the
coastguards spoke to the American with us; there
were several boats, launches, and skiffs anchored,
awaiting the order to enter; everything had come
closer to us: the lights, the American music, the
flag of the United States; I looked at the stars
sunk in the night, I took a deep breath, they
were like the stars in my country; we were given
permission to enter at 9:00 that night; as
President Carter said, welcoming those Cubans
who wanted to come to this great nation with open
arms, that is how the multitudes welcomed us,
with open arms; on land there were American
soldiers with wheelchairs for the old or infirm
that disembarked; we felt welcomed, surprised at
so much fellowship being extended to us who
arrived bearing the stamp of scum; the women and
children started to descend, helped down by the

soldiers; the doctors checked to see whether
there were any ill people; those that were waiting
on land shook our hands, they hugged us, they
kissed us; many of those who had arrived were
without shoes, shirts, showing their prison
tattoos, set into the skin with a needle and the
smoke from the burnt ends of toothbrushes; I had
watched them doing tattoos, they collected the
smoke inside a tin until it formed a crust, they
added a bit of water to this crust and used this
to make the ink for the tattoos; my compatriots
walked about now with their painted bodies, like
walking newspapers; we lined up in Indian file;
the Cubans who came to meet us asked, what
province are you from? are you from Las Villas?
let's see, is there someone from Luyanó amongst
you? they gave us sodas, cigarettes, and food; we
hadn't even finished what they'd given us when
they were offering us more; they took us to some
offices where they asked us for some information;
many did not have a passport or any type of
identification; many changed their names and
their surnames; nearby, on an altar, the Virgin
of Our Lady of Charity, patron saint of Cuba, a
beautiful image illuminated by candles; also, a
statue of our Apostle, José Martí; it seemed to
me that the statue of Antonio Maceo Grajales was
missing, Bronze Titan, a Mambí warrior who had
carried Independence from San Antonio to Maisí;
why is his statue missing? after giving our
details we were taken to other offices; I'm still
moved by this treatment accorded us by so many
Cubans that had come here years before and who
now received us like brothers; I saw for the
first time the possibility of being responsible

for my own actions as a free man; it was fabulous
to see the North American products with their
labels so foreign to us, everything was very
strange, especially the red carpet treatment; new
faces, unknown laughter, everything occurred as
if in a dream; we arrived at a restaurant where
our compatriots welcomed us with exquisite
delicacies; the restaurant, huge, the Cuban food
so abundant that it was impossible for us to eat
everything they gave us; at the end of dinner,
coffee and cigarettes; when we left the restaurant
there were several buses from a company called
Trailways; the driver, a black American, was very
nice to us; our joy ran through us like a river
that was overflowing; but at the moment when I
thought I had conquered the sun, I arrived at a
volcano about to erupt; at first sight Cayo Hueso
seemed to be a paradise; the driver slowed down
so that we could see the streets, most of them
deserted, the bars empty; we reached the outskirts
and a few metres away, there was the sea; I
thought, how many shipwrecks from the flotilla is
it hiding; the bus stopped in front of some large
wooden buildings surrounded by fences about eight
feet high, a control tower, a small landing strip;
a guard spoke to us in Spanish, ladies and
gentlemen, if there are any families amongst you,
could they please move to one side, and single
gentlemen please collect here, he pointed to his
left, he continued speaking: the single men will
go to the tents, the families are to go to that
building over there to wait for their relations
to collect them or to await the aeroplane's
departure; he stopped talking, we headed, in
Indian file, to the tents; rows of beds with

quilts, the tents were quite wide; in each one there were more than one hundred men; we start lying down on the beds; several acquaintances greet me, one comes up to me, what a place, *compa*, how was your trip? ok, I guess, Tony; just ok, nothing more, or do you still feel a little scared? no, *compadre*, I never felt afraid, it's just that I'm exhausted from the trip, someone else addresses Tony: my friend, what's that scarface like? what scarface? that one, said the young guy pointing at me while he spoke, it seems that he adapted just as soon as he smelt Yony Land; forget it, buddy, I haven't adapted, the ones who have adapted are the whores like you; this guy had already pulled a knife on me in Cuba and I pulled my 32 pistol that I always carried with me on him; when I insulted him I took a step backwards to prepare myself; he raised his fist but before he could beat me, Orlando stopped him and peppered him with punches; within a few seconds the young guy was lying on the ground, out for the count; a friend came to help him, he headed for Orlando, I didn't let him get that far, I punched him in his stomach, doubling him over, quickly I pulled him by the bottoms of his trousers so that he fell backwards, he moved, trying to defend himself; I fell on him and started beating him with a piece of pole that I picked up from the ground; Mede! Mede, my brother, leave him now, leave him, Orlando shouted at me while he separated us, pulling me by the collar of my shirt; another voice at my side shouts, here comes the guard, hurry up or they'll put you in jail; I stopped hitting him, when I got up I saw my compatriots reviving the one who had fought

with Orlando; someone else arrived with a can of
Coca-Cola full of water and threw it in the face
of the man laying on the ground; a soldier, some
distance away from me, walks towards us to inspect
my adversary; Orlando points to another guard
that is heading our way: let's go, Mede, hurry
up, this scene is turning ugly; I followed
Orlando who was walking quickly towards another
tent; we went inside, we lay down with shoes and
everything, we covered ourselves from head to
toe; Orlando agreed to keep watch, until, Mede,
they've taken those two away, they took them in
a car; Orlando, now we're definitely in the shit
if those two *enfermas* tell on us; Orlando tries
to calm me down, don't worry, brother, what we
have to do is try to get out of this place as
soon as possible; that's easy to say, but how are
we going to get out of here? I don't know, Mede,
but there has to be a way, because it would be
terrible if things fell apart now; I think about
what he's just said to me, and yes, that would be
an incredible tragedy, at this stage, to end up
in prison again; I got up, I started walking
around the cot where Orlando was lying; a few
metres away from us, several refugees are talking
softly; others look at us trying to make out what
we are saying; at the other end of the tent some
guards are talking to a number of refugees, I
don't know if they're asking about us; Orlando
speaks to those nearest us, *caballero*, make sure
you don't sing because if you do, even if it is
in front of the guards, I'll send you to your
Guardian Angel; a huge silence fell interrupted
by a loudspeaker calling those refugees whose
families had come to fetch them; I wanted to

support Orlando: anyone who says that we were the
two who were fighting, is looking for big trouble;
one of those present came up to us, *compadres*,
don't worry about that, I'm with you, and anyone
who dares will have Cheo to deal with; I held out
my hand, thank you very much, Cheo; this is the
first time I've ever seen this Cheo but this type
of environment is like that, if you show them you
are strong, they immediately want to join you;
Cheo strikes a pose as though to give a long
talk, he looks at everyone to reassure them: I
have never known fear, they know me in all the
prisons in Cuba and it's all the same to me to
land in jail here or die with anyone, I'm jinxed;
another in the group joins us, he speaks to the
rest, there are many of us here that know Cheo
Rutina and he's a friend of mine, come on, come,
if he's on the side of these two guys I am too;
three guards approach us, and one starts to ask
us in perfect Spanish: which of you knows who
attacked those two young boys that were taken to
hospital? I would like you to cooperate with us,
nothing will happen to the attacker, we only want
to speak to him; when he finished speaking he
looked at each one of us waiting for someone to
say something, but to no avail; Orlando looked at
me twice and immediately I understood what he
wanted to tell me; El Cheo decided to speak, none
of us knows anything, check with the one who
fought; the guard tried to convince us, it's
unbelievable that you should behave like this,
men should be forthright; I took a step towards
him, and if we don't know what it is that you
want us to say? Orlando took me by the shoulders
and when I looked towards him he was winking at

me, I stopped; the guard insisted, one of you has
to know something, you're not blind; Cheo steps
forward, you're the one who's blind, friend; he
let the words out while frowning and showing a
platinum tooth that shone in the light of the
electric bulb; show some respect or I'll lock you
up right now, and more to the point, I'm sure you
were the one that attacked those two boys; Cheo
gets even madder, either this queer has gone
crazy or he's never heard of Cheo Rutina; while
still speaking, he throws himself at the guard
but he doesn't have time to do anything, at that
moment, in the blink of an eye, the other guards
immobilize him by handcuffing him, I had never
seen a guard move so quickly; Orlando wanted to
intervene, but I stopped him; stand still, or do
you want to stay in the shit? now that Cheo has
cornered the market, leave it; but, Mede, it's
just that it's our problem, it's not his; look,
brother, this was a diversion, they're not going
to do anything to Cheo; I turn to the guard but
Cheo won't let me get to him: *compadre*, leave it
to me, I'll sort it out with these jokers, don't
you know that it's better to go by yourself rather
than with two others? as you like, my friend,
remember that they're all in cahoots and you
won't get anywhere with them; I thought that when
he heard me he would realise that he should stop
shooting his mouth off, but he continued shouting,
yes, I know that this is a huge force but I'm
Cheo and I don't give way to anybody; three
guards walk at his side without paying attention
to the rubbish he was sprouting in his prison
language; one of those who had said that he was
Cheo's friend expressed his admiration, now

that's a man, that Cheo is a real man; Orlando gestured to me, I followed him out the tent, we stopped in the grounds next to a water tank that was there for our use; Mede, it's not right that we should leave Cheo on his own; well, and what did you want to do, start a fight with the soldiers? no, brother, but we could have said that we were the ones they were looking for; I don't see it like that, Orlando, because, in any case, he would have tried to go with us and for my part, I've had enough of being imprisoned; I came here to try and become someone else, not the troublemaker I was in Cuba and if we can get away with this, why insist? you're right, Mede, but it bothers me that someone else should pay for what I've done; look there, Orlando, they're lining up, let's go and see what's happening; we walk up to a group of people lined up in Indian file like always; when we arrive the group marches out of the door through which, one hour earlier, we had entered; a guard dressed in a camouflage uniform brought three crates of Coca Cola and started sharing them out amongst us; then he started talking to us about life in the United States; this guard was the son of Puerto Ricans and had been born in the United States; they called another group that were taken away by buses; they didn't call out our names; the guards talk to us in sign language as if we were deaf and dumb, but in reality, we were because we couldn't say one word; the only one who knew English was Orlando because in Fishing School they had to learn to speak English if they wanted to graduate as officers responsible for loading cargo; three homosexuals cause the guards some amusement, one

starts to dance; the other refugees sing for
them; a guard brought a box, a refugee started
drumming on the box and the others started
clapping; soon there was a party going on in the
tents, as if we were celebrating our victory; I
forgot my problems, and gave in to this unexpected
happiness, I felt as though we were bringing
ourselves closer to our land through song; I
return to reality with the call to board the bus
that will take us to the airport; I'm overcome by
a sadness that is subdued by my hope of being
free; the starry sky, the moon losing itself
behind the clouds, she appears and disappears
among them like an actress on stage to offer us,
her extraordinary audience, her harmonious drama;
seated in the bus, I'm surprised by Cheo's voice:
and, my friend, so now you can see that nobody
dies, least of all now, I'm Cheo and even the
cops respect me; yes, Cheo, one can see that,
but, tell me, how did you get free? Tony asks
him, stopping near Cheo's seat; it was nothing,
Tony, you know I'm a slippery bastard and I can
escape through the eye of a needle; yes, Cheo,
you're the best, Tony assures him starting to
laugh; the two characters continue their
conversation, both seated now in the same seat;
the bus pulls away, a vision of empty, lit streets
reaches us; we hear the noise of straggling cars;
Orlando speaks to me, how beautiful this city is,
Mede, I'd like to be walking these streets right
now; I continue watching the lights that appear
out of the darkness, I answer without looking at
him, yes, it would be nice to walk these streets;
I feel quite overcome, I never thought that Cayo
Hueso would appear to us in the night, as if out

of a fairy story, as if produced in a fraction of
a second by an act of magic; we arrive at the
airport in 35 minutes, at the entrance, a soldier
stands guard; a military car approaches us,
uniformed men wearing air force regalia get out
of it, they escort us to a nearby hanger, we
enter, they order us to sit down with a warning
that we mustn't smoke because it would be
dangerous; the hanger is full of aeroplane parts
and an almost totally dismantled helicopter; on
the repair workbenches: propellers, pieces of
engines; outside, on the floodlight runway: the
control tower, several planes, helicopters, three
small planes, so small that they surprise me, I'd
never seen anything like this; the escorts were
fairly friendly to us but every now and then they
told us to sit down again as the way we were
sitting was becoming uncomfortable and sometimes
we moved about; we stayed like this until five in
the morning when we were told to stand up for
inspection; each of us, after being searched, had
to go up to the military personnel who had brought
boxes from which they issued nylon bags labelled
in English; the contents of these bags were for
personal hygiene: a toothbrush, a tube of Colgate
toothpaste, an electric razor; we boarded an
aeroplane that seemed beautiful to me; its seats,
for three people; I sat down near the window and
Orlando, next to me; a woman's voice tells us
about the trip in broken Spanish, with terrible
pronunciation, we can hardly understand what she
is trying to tell us; an elegantly dressed man
walks up and down the aeroplane; I say he must be
the plane's guard because I watched him help a
girl fasten her seat belt; when he bent over, I

saw the pistol he had in his belt; a short time
passes, we take off, the air hostess instructs us
to stay in our respective seats; I fell asleep
until Orlando's voice woke me up: Mede, it's
morning! it was true, the sun was pushing its way
through the clouds to give us a beautiful morning
in which we could make out buildings that looked
like toys, rivers, lakes, mountains, forests,
which I surveyed from my great height; the
aeroplane made headway through occasional air
pockets; my companions slept off their exhaustion
after overcoming their fear of flying for the
first time; for me this was nothing new as I had
boarded several planes to travel from Havana into
the country's interior; Orlando was still talking
to me, soon I interrupted him to go to the
bathroom on the plane; I looked at myself in the
mirror, it was like looking at a ghost; I washed
my hands, my face, I watched the grime run into
the water; I inspected my filthy clothes; I left
the bathroom; to get back to my seat I had to
wake up my companion; I'm assailed by fleeting
images; my loved ones, a past which leaves a
bitter taste; I felt myself crying quietly;
suddenly I felt myself tense up, trying to locate
myself in time; I realised that everything was
taking place high up in the air, and the earlier
images quickly disappeared; I found the two air
hostesses attractive, one of them offers me a
cigarette, she asks me several questions which I
don't understand and which I leave unanswered, I
see her walk off with a beautiful swing, I keep
watching her body, her hips, while I remember her
incredibly blue eyes; attention, attention,
ladies and gentlemen, fasten your seat belts, in

a few moments, we will be landing, we thank you for flying with us on this happy voyage; the voice of the air hostess switches off again; from my height I see a river that seems to have no end, crossed from time to time by bridges; an immense road flowing with cars which, seen from here, become minute; everything mixed up with fragments of nature, a blue sky, a lake, a hill; we're descending, it seems to me that we're going to nose-dive and crash on the runway, we land to start the journey into this new life, unknown to us, known to other human beings; ladies and gentlemen, your journey has come to an end, welcome to the State of Pennsylvania, welcome to your new life; in a few moments you will board the buses that will take you to a fort in Indiantown Gap where you will be processed and released to rejoin your friends and relations, thank you very much; the person speaking to you is the F.B.I. representative chosen to welcome you on behalf of the Governor of this state; we wish you a happy stay in the fort and may God grant you quick assimilation into this society; the speech was made by a voice that remained foreign to all of us while speaking perfect Spanish; on the runway, there were several aeroplanes; the control tower with its strange construction came as a surprise to us; we left the plane in an orderly fashion; several military types that may have been police lined up on either side of the stairs in two lines leading from the plane and extending to the bus which we were to board; while I walked, I felt a cold that I had never before experienced, I was frozen right down to the innermost part of my body; in the bus, the

cold abated a bit; we were given some information
pamphlets written in Spanish with photos of the
camp and an explication of the procedure to
follow when we arrived; we were given something
to read about Cambodian and Vietnamese refugees
who, five years ago, had inhabited the fort where
we were going to stay; we read something about
the Americans in this State, how they lived;
there were references to the Puerto Rican
population and a number of things that were new
to us; Orlando settled himself down at my side to
tell me his plans for the future; I was scared,
that fear that I always feel when confronting the
future; I always say that when faced with the
future we are like illiterates facing an open
book that we can't understand; the chain of buses
runs near the runway looking for the exit from
the airport; almost at the exit, there's a huge
factory; the houses in the city are single
stories, all of brick with a few wooden sections;
everything's so beautiful; the cars pass us with
heady speed leaving us behind; the signs, forming,
with letters we know, words that we can't
understand; Orlando can't contain himself:
brother, how fantastic this world is; yes, it's
all like a dream to me, a movie, I reply, moved;
a quick inventory of the events in my life takes
me to another dimension where I stay for I don't
know how long until Orlando's voice pulled me
back to this moment, Mede! Mede! you're bewitched,
what are you thinking about? his eyes find mine,
find the eyes of that being who at that moment
was far away from me walking down other roads,
find the eyes of that being that escapes and
leaves me intangible, like a memory; solidity

returns to me, I speak to him in a voice that
becomes mine; I try and explain to him, it was
almost as though I had just been born, as if they
had pushed me into the world leaving behind a
sour taste, the painful experience that
accompanies me; I become engrossed in the scenery
without allowing Orlando's voice to interrupt me:
don't talk rubbish, Mede, is the journey making
you feel ill? I let myself be carried by the
movement of the bus that was taking us to two-
story houses or barracks, made of wood, painted
white; soon we realised that we were in a
miniature city composed of white houses, green
lawns, surrounded by mountains; one can see a few
pedestrians, some cars crossing the streets with
their laments rising like a protest at their
relentless labour; some butterflies which, from
the window of the bus, seem to me to be strangely
free playing amongst the flowers; the first buses
start turning into a small street leaving the
avenue behind; on either side, the white barracks;
as I start asking myself what they are used for,
I recognise some of my countrymen who are already
living in the fort; there is a small sign on
which I can make out the inscription "Zone 5"
which marks an area where only Cuban married
couples with their children are seen; the buses
move away from the street we travelled briefly by
turning right and stopping next to some barracks
in the men's zone, lines of men, groups of men,
men walking, talking, there is not one woman to
be seen, not one child; a woman appears on the
bus and speaks to us in perfect Spanish: welcome
to your new home; in a few minutes you'll be
given breakfast and then go on to Immigration;

they'll give you a card which will indicate the zone where you'll live and they'll take your photo; does anyone have any questions? a profound silence, no-one asks anything; after waiting for a few moments for our answer: you may start getting off the bus and should follow me; we trusted her friendly gesture and began alighting from the bus starting with those at the back and, once outside, we lined up; once we were all off the bus, it moved off, the driver stuck his hand out the window to wave goodbye as he drove away; we were temporarily housed in a barracks with beds, mattresses, wardrobes, all very different to the places I had seen used as shelters; the bathrooms were well looked after, you could feel the hygiene everywhere; a compatriot pulled a funny face and started to delve into the wardrobes to see what they contained, all he found was a woman's change of underwear which he shook in the air while shouting, look what I found, now I have something to fantasize about and saying this, he put the clothes in the pocket of his trousers; hey, friend, lend that to me if you can, I also have needs, one of the group shouted at him; forget it, this isn't something you lend; compa, don't be so mean to your friend as we're all in this together, intervened a third; the voice of the woman who was our guide could be heard from the entrance to the barracks: gentlemen, it's now time for breakfast but I want you to line up outside; the two that had started the argument continued arguing over the clothes once the woman had disappeared from the doorway; oh, so you're not going to give me anything, me, who has pulled so many strings to stop them busting your ass!

you're too much of a whore to be looking after me
and when we get where we're going I'll show you
who's boss; the other raises his voice and makes
expansive gestures with his hands, showing his
silver tooth: hey, look at the little girl, *Yuma*
has made her brave, but to me she's still the
same; Pepe el Cojo goes up to them to stop the
fight that's about to start: why don't we leave
this argument until we get there, now behave
yourselves properly like the good boys that you
are because I know all about you two and it's a
sad and embarrassing story; Pepe el Cojo, a man
of about 38, has been in prison since he was a
child, he claims to know everything about everyone
around him and when he spoke everyone shut up,
because maybe Pepe el Cojo really does know
everything; we start leaving the shelter and when
I reached the woman who was our guide, I wanted
to know, tell me, and forgive me for bothering
you, what country are you from? I'm from Puerto
Rico, why? she replied smiling; nothing, out of
curiosity; um, could you lend me one of those
towels? I'm very cold; yes, with pleasure, here
you are, keep it, although they'll give all of
you towels when you get to your respective areas
or zones; the white towel that she offered me had
U.S.A. written on it in black letters; I threw it
over my shoulders, thank you very much! glad to
be of service, is there anything else you need?
she said to me, showing her perfect teeth; no,
there's nothing else I need and I don't know how
to repay you for doing me this favour; it's no
favour, it's my job to help you all; let's go and
have breakfast as you've spent enough time going
without in your country; she started walking, I

followed her while thinking about the hunger and
the misfortune that we had suffered in that
country that I had left transformed into a grave
for the living; I felt a deep awareness of freedom
within this new country where I could think of
myself with a sense of pride, where I could
express myself without my voice breaking; we
started to walk to the dining room filled with a
tremendous happiness, anticipating the moment
when we would satisfy the hunger which had been
with us for some time; on the way we made out the
barracks which served as the Immigration Office
where lines of refugees that had arrived before
us awaited their turn to be interviewed by the
people from Immigration; in the dining room, we
headed, in Indian file, to the counters where
they gave us little boxes containing a variety of
provisions, the people who attended us were
Americans, all as white as snow from a lack of
sun; in the dining room there were several tables
with their respective chairs, as if they were
about to serve a dinner to an important delegation;
when I sat down next to Orlando I couldn't decide
which of the tins to open first until Orlando
decided for me, Mede, give me one of these tins
so that I can open it for you as I can see that
you don't know where to start; I let him take one
of the tins to open it; it would seem that these
rations are used by the army at times of war or
during manoeuvres since all the boxes are olive
green and come equipped with everything: chewing
gum, opener, matches, napkins and different cans;
do you like this one, Mede? I heard Orlando say
while offering me a tin of processed meat; yes,
exactly that one, I replied reacting almost

automatically; I began devouring the contents
using the plastic cutlery that came with the box;
in the dining room it was almost impossible to
hear what we were trying to say as my compatriots
had set up a tremendous commotion; a man from our
table brought all of us coffee; there was no
sugar in the coffee, but the box contained little
packets of coffee, sugar, powdered milk, salt,
powdered chocolate; all of the provisions tasted
delicious to me; I got up out of my seat and went
to a fridge containing milk, I took three glasses
and carried them back to the table; I remembered
the rations: children up to six years of age are
allowed evaporated milk and if they want litres
of milk, a long paper chase has to be pursued
with the doctor in charge of approving a milk
diet; I remembered the protest made by the
comedians called Los Tarados on their radio
programme: what is the lowest act a president can
commit? to starve the people and then provide a
free funeral; this little joke sent the two
comedians to prison and nothing has been heard of
them since; those in the military forces enjoy
certain privileges, but when the Angolan thing
came, many of them refused to go, others went so
that they could have a better standard of living
when they came back; when they returned they
found the same misery, their apathy towards
Angola increased, since then participants in
international missions are not told that they are
leaving, nor where they are going, they're not
allowed to inform their families when they're
notified about their departure; after a very
filling breakfast we head for the Immigration
queue; Orlando and I are the last in line; a

Puerto Rican man comes up to the queue, we need
two volunteers for a small job; he started to
look at those present to see who'd agree to do
the work; two of my compatriots stepped forward;
the man speaks to them, thank you for your
cooperation, the job involves picking up the
papers and cigarette butts that are lying around
this building, it's just that the mayor of the
city is here and we want him to take away a good
impression of the place; saying this he headed
for the door going into the building and
disappeared; the two volunteers started muttering
under their breaths, something that I couldn't
make out, and immediately they began collecting
the papers and cigarette butts that they found;
someone in the line, with an incredible look of
disgust, protests, look at those two, they thought
they were going to do something else and that's
why they offered; someone else stops him, you
don't have to pull that face to say something
like that; yes my friend, because these people
think that us Cubans are just garbage collectors,
not so? if it were me I'd tell him to pick it up
himself; I go up to Orlando whom I notice is a
little sad, what's the matter, my brother?
nothing, I was just thinking about my people back
in Cuba; he replied, lowering his head and looking
at the ground as if looking to it for an answer
or solution to his problems; don't think so much,
what's done, is done, you can't turn back, I said
to him while taking him by the shoulders to make
him look up; I know, Mede, that you can't turn
back, but in this country nothing is going to be
easy; so, you were thinking about this country
where we've been sent as undesireables, expelled

from our own country? well, actually I was
thinking about the victory I've won in coming to
the U.S.A.; yes, Orlando, but remember that this
victory is just the start of a new battle; he
shook my hand, and reaffirmed to me: but I've
won! remember, Orlando, that a winning card in a
game of cards depends on the other card you're
dealt, for now this victory is just the beginning
of another battle and it's not that I'm as
pessimistic as you think I am, it's just that I'm
in touch with reality; Orlando repeats his words
with a childlike expression on his face,
displaying the purity of his way of thinking to
me; it's our turn to go into Immigration; almost
all their employees are from Puerto Rico, we pass
through various departments where they ask us
questions and we fill out forms; when we finished
in one department, the employee that has assisted
us pointed: follow the arrow, please! we follow
the paper arrows stuck to the wall, in a straight
line or bent to indicate the next place where we
must continue filling out forms; they take photos
of us, they take our finger prints, it's a real
procedure that they're putting us through, but
they explained to us that this was the only way
of legalizing our entry into the country; at the
exit there were some buses waiting for us to take
us to our respective zones; when boarding the bus
we had to show a card on which our photo, our
name, and the number of the barracks in Zone 12
appeared; a woman who was going to act as our
interpreter boarded the bus with us, gentlemen, I
would like you to remain in your assigned seats
throughout the journey and I ask you to maintain
discipline here, when you get to your zone you

will be issued with bed sheets and items for your personal hygiene, thank you; our interpreter then began reviewing our cards or labels that would serve as our identification in this refuge; I started analysing the fact that although they expelled us from our country as scum we were a reflection of that society because most of us had been raised in that system and knew no other method of government; on our way to the zone that was to be our new home, we came across several soldiers who marched along the road and others who ran towards them; our convoy consisted of two identical buses painted in yellow colour; Orlando, when I get to my quarters I'm going to try and find out if my family has come and to see where they've sent El Chévere; Orlando remained deep in thought watching the cars coming and going; yes, I think that's a good idea, maybe you can see him here, what will you do if you see Niurka? will you go back to her? Orlando stared me straight in the eye and for the first time I felt his look wound me; I considered his question, working out an answer about this woman for whom I had suffered so bitterly in captivity, longing for her warmth during these 6 months and 27 days we had been separated; I heard Orlando insist, don't you want to talk about her? the truth is that I don't know what I'd do if I saw her again, it all depends on what she tells me, if I were to tell you I don't love her, I'd be lying to you; brother, you'll forget all this when you meet an American woman and be with her, because you forget one love with another, I also want to throw into obscurity the memories I have of the woman I was with before being arrested and I shouldn't need to tell you that because you already know the whole story; while saying this he became a little downcast; I saw in him the brother I was never able to have at my side, my father's other two sons have nothing to do with me, they're integrated into the system, strangers to me, perhaps meeting them would be a meeting of enemies; Orlando reminds me that the day Niurka came to visit me she told me that she might come over before me, but in truth I doubt that she has because the father of her daughter has to approve Yardely's departure and God alone knows where he is, maybe in Oriente; little by little I changed the subject away from this painful topic of conversation that brought with it a sense of something faded, like a solitary flower that brings to mind the silence of tombs; we turn into a street bearing a sign from which we can easily make out that "Zone 12" is its final destination, my new home or my new hell, because I know that I won't be dealing with school kids, we're beings who carry with us a bitter taste and now we have to fight against the distance that separates us from our families; in prison, we waited day after day for the moment when Visitors' Day would arrive so that we could see them, now they are out of our reach; a group of compatriots comes out to meet us, many look into the bus's interior searching for some relation or friend; amongst them are a number a acquaintances of mine, one called Teleforo, the great destroyer of young men, surrounded by his teleforitos as he calls the boys who submit to his desires; many a time I heard Teleforo say that he was better off in prison than out on the street because in prison he had everything

provided and he could enjoy his teleforitos; a
military type boards the bus, he speaks to us in
Spanish: this is the zone where you will live
until you are able to locate your relatives or
friends and, in this way, integrate into society;
one of the things I ask of you is that you help
to maintain order and that you take the advice of
your counsellors; each barracks will have a
counsellor you will elect for yourselves, although
the person who is given the responsibility must
be able to speak English; in a few moments you
will be issued with bed sheets and items for your
personal hygiene and a box of cigarettes; every
day your counsellor will come to the warehouse to
collect the cigarettes allotted to you; in a few
moments we will take you to the quarters indicated
on your identification cards, we recommend that
you look after these cards carefully; his speech
ended with a thank you and may God watch over
you; I thought that maybe, after so many years,
God would remember us and would begin watching
over us a little more or maybe would forget about
these few hundred undesireables, these men
expelled from the land that taught them to be
undesireables so that, later, it could shout in
their faces that they were the scum of the
country; a few steps away from the bus was a man
with a stick, he had been crippled in prison by
a knife wound, at that moment he was laughing at
something someone had said to him, but his
laughter came out bitter, as if it were more of a
reflection of his pain; we were ordered to alight
from the bus to collect our dining cards and we
were told to return to our respective buses
afterwards; these cards were made for us while we

waited, you had only to show your identification
card; we boarded our bus again which then took us
to the warehouse where we were given fairly large
nylon bags; our luggage was now becoming somewhat
cumbersome, and to think that a few hours ago we
owned nothing; from the window of the bus I began
spotting quite a few acquaintances, most of whom
had been travelling through friendly countries,
as we called Cuba's many prisons; when someone is
released and bumps into a friend, immediately he
is asked, were you travelling through friendly
countries? or, if not, where were you? in Canada?
a military type boarded the bus and told us that
we should elect our counsellor and that whomever
we elected had to get off the bus so that they
could issue him with a card that would acknowledge
him as a counsellor, he would have to take that
card with him when he went to fetch what was
needed for the barracks where we were to be
installed; we started asking our compatriots if
they could speak English; Orlando, why don't you
accept the position? no, I don't like giving
orders to anyone nor have I come here to look for
trouble with anyone; but Orlando, I don't think
you'll be looking for trouble, no-one seems
troublesome; Orlando continued to refuse until a
man of about 40, called Pablo, agreed to be the
counsellor; of about average height, well covered,
Pablo seemed a decent person, without any
indication of having been in prison; everyone
present greeted our counsellor with delight; we
arrived at our double story, white-painted
barracks; it seems that this is a more systematic
life than the one we lived in prison; for someone
coming from prison, life here seems wonderful,

it's all a case of getting used to it; we got off
the buses, we entered our barracks to choose our
beds set out in twos, one on top of the other;
these beds look terribly inviting, but first, a
bath is needed, to rid myself of this sour odour;
Orlando took the bottom bunk, I took the upper, I
prefer the top bunk because anyone visiting sits
on the bottom bunk; we start emptying the contents
of our bags: two quilts, two sheets, one
pillowcase, one towel, a packet of Camel
cigarettes, a box of tobacco mixed with apple
peal, a bar of soap, a razor; Orlando had to help
me make my bed which is a little too high for me;
the bathrooms are impeccable with newly painted
doors; in the bathroom a number of my compatriots
are washing themselves, bathing, the bath looked
very inviting; I surveyed the tattoos, I read
their slogans: "a gentleman is a hat, a walking
stick and pair of gloves;" "I'll swop a party
for a wake;" "I'll kiss you and scold you at the
same time;" "I'm only who I am;" "friend of what;"
"mother, give me strength because guts I have;"
"don't talk to me about friendship;" "tell me,
what do you want?" "my friends are the dead, my
parents: sadness and loneliness;" others displayed
a picture of Saint Barbara; initials on hands, on
fingers, on feet, serpents with the head of a
woman, tattoos in mouths, on eyelids, where, when
they were closed, one could read "I see you;"
between the thumb and index finger, the five dice
dots that the pickpockets use; in prison, a friend
offered to tattoo me, I rejected his invitation
because tattoos are a burden; I left the bathroom
and headed for my bed, most of the people that
were to be found in the barracks were putting

their things away in individual wardrobes painted grey, made of metal; my body was finished; I took my towel and the soap and went to take a shower; Orlando was in the doorway to the exit, preoccupied, lost in thought; I went on my way without calling him; it bothered me that I didn't have any clean clothes to change into, not even underpants; I found the shower freezing, I turned the other tap, boiling water came out that made me jump to one side so as not to burn myself, at last I managed to regulate the temperature; the water draining away is filthy, full of the grime from my body; I had to soap myself three times to clean myself a little; I washed my underpants which were stained with grease, it seems that they must have been stained in the boat when I sat on the ground, my other items of clothing are also full of grease, dust and God only knows how many other things; I left the bathroom, and spread out my underpants outside, on the grass that grew near the barracks because the sun didn't reach the wash lines; I sat down on a rock; I allowed my mind to slide down the narrow, muddy road of my memories, my anguish began to find its voice, I started calling my mother, my daughter, Yuny, my sister, many times, repeatedly, but their fragile images soon dissolved leaving me to this insistent and terrible loneliness; I see myself reflected in the quiet breathing of the grass as an indistinct being, visited by beings from other worlds who come to my side to leave their voiceless word so that the touch of my skin doesn't wilt the flowers

GLOSSARY

ahijada - goddaughter. According to African tradition, when someone is made a saint, that is to say, when the energy of a deity or *orisha* is implanted in his or her head, the neophyte becomes the godchild of a godmother and a godfather known respectively as the *madrina de santo* and *padrino de santo*. Depending on which orisha is involved, the godchild is said to have been made a saint in *Changó*, in *Obatalá*, etc. A birthday indicates the number of years that person has been a saint. On the birthday of a goddaughter, her godmother offers the beat of *batá* drums to the saint. The drums are beaten by special *batá* drummers.

antisocial - A common accusation. When you want to sent someone to jail, you accuse him of being antisocial or hostile. The accused is charged under the Law of Dangerousness and the usual sentence (which may be arbitrarily and repeatedly extended) is one of four years.

Algayú - The father of *Changó*. According to other sources, he also appears under the names *Argayú* and *Aggayú*, lord of rivers and savannas, represented by St Christopher. *Algayú* is a huge orisha.

babalao - A priest who officiates in African religious rituals. He determines, through divination, what saint should be made. The shells that reveal the prophecy are thrown on the Board of Orula (the god of divination).

becados -Young people selected by the government to receive all-inclusive scholarships to further their studies or to learn a trade.

breva **or** *tupamaro* - A cigarette made from whatever is at hand: newspaper, mattress stuffing, etc.

caballero! - Sir! 1) An exclamation used by the speaker to gain the attention of those around him. 2) An exclamation which may indicate complaint or surprise: "*Caballero*, imagine this happening to me"; "*Caballero*, who could have known that this would happen".

chain - Massive transfer of prisoners from one section of the prison to another.

Changó - The orisha or god of virility, fire, and lightning. Wears red and is represented by St Barbara. When this Saint mounts the medium (when he enters the body of the medium), he makes suggestive and obscene allusions to his virility. He is a womanising and violent orisha. Very powerful.

combatiente - soldier, trooper; sir

Combinado del Este - A prison in Eastern Havana.

command - The power that one prisoner may exert in the corridors of the prison. The prisoner who wields this power is known as the commander.

Community, Members of the Community - Cubans who began to immigrate to the

United States as a result of the Revolution. The official term used to refer to them at the time was that of *gusanos* (worms). When flights to Cuba opened up and exiled Cubans could visit Cuba, the term *"gusanos"* was replaced with the designation "Members of the Community" so as not to offend these suppliers of dollars.

compa - friend, comrade. Probably an apocope of compadre.

cordon - The wardens that guard the prison from the outside.

Dangerousness; the Law of Dangerousness - A law which governs the arrest and imprisonment of those considered to be dangerous to the regime. The usual sentence for dangerousness is four years.

Eleguá - The orisha of paths, he guards the crossroads, the savanna and the mountains. His nature may be that of a naughty child or it may turn malevolent. One must keep him happy so as not to get on his bad side as he possesses the key to destiny. The santería celebrations always open with a hymn to *Eleguá*. His emblem is the branch of a tree in the shape of a shepherd's crook; his colours: red and black. He is represented by the Holy Child of Atocha.

El Norte - the North; the name many Cubans give to the United States.

enferma - Pejorative expression used to designate the passive male homosexual.

guaguancó - A typical Cuban dance performed to the beat of a drum.

Guanajay - Guanajay Prison; originally a jail for women, now inhabited by men.

gusanos - Worms. Pejorative expression used at official level and by the general populous with regard to political dissidents.

itá - The reading the *babalao* makes about the future of the person to be initiated, known as the *asentado*. The reading includes those things from which the *asentado* must abstain throughout his or her life once a secret name, given in the Lucumí language, has been assigned to that person. "I never knew your saint name, the one that came to you from the *itá*, from the mat sprinkled with Cowrie shells".

Iyabó - A person who has been initiated as son or daughter of a saint must wear white for one year and must not use his or her own name, rather, he or she should be addressed as *Iyabó*. Once initiated as son or daughter of a saint, the Iyabó sits on a throne, the same colour as that representing the saint or orisha, for seven days. On each of these days a different ritual is performed. "I imagine you, dressed in white for the seven days you sit on your throne and then, already transformed into *Iyabó*, wearing white for a year".

jaba - A large bag, usually made from woven fan palm fibre. Prisoners are allowed to have family members and friends bring them a *jaba* of food and other items of immediate necessity on certain days.

jeba - A woman. In using the term *jeba*, men define a woman according to her sexual function. For example, the term may be used to refer to a woman that a man would like to have at his disposal for his sexual gratification.

KM - A weapon, a machine gun.

lancheros - Those people that escaped or tried to escape from Cuba on motorboats.

Lucumí - 1) Afro-Cubans of Yoruba descent; 2) a language learnt and passed on by initiates into *Santería*.

necklaces - Made from beads of a colour which corresponds to the Saint with whom one is working: white for *Obatalá*; blue for *Yemayá*, etc.

Nuevo Amanecer - (Literally - New Sunrise). A prison for women.

Obatalá - An old orisha, shaky and unsure of step, but with the ability to transform himself into a young warrior. He is the immaculate god, the compassionate one. His colour is white, symbolizing purity. He is represented by Our Lady of Mercy.

Ogún - A warrior orisha, lord of iron. He is represented by St Peter.

Operation Inca - The widespread arrest of all those that approached the Peruvian Embassy with the intention of seeking asylum. Many of these people, considered to be 'hostile' or 'scum,' were taken from their homes and sent out via the port of

Mariel on what was later known in the United States as the 'Freedom Flotilla'. A large percentage of those forced to leave Cuba (coming from their homes, from prisons or from hospitals for the mentally ill) had their passports falsely marked to indicate that they had sought asylum from the Peruvian Embassy.

oquendos - sticks used in karate.

orishas - Gods or saints with the virtues and vices of men. They are the intermediaries between humans and *Olofi*, the supreme being and creator.

Orula - The diviner orisha, he possesses the diviner's board that originally belonged to *Obatalá* and *Changó*. The board passed to *Orula* when *Changó* gave it to him in exchange for the elegance that *Orula*, in spite of his advanced age, displayed when he danced. *Orula* is represented by St Francis. He is also known by the names of *Orúmila* and *Orúmbila*. His colours are yellow and green. The *babalaos* work with this orisha in their function as diviners.

Oshún - The orisha of sweet waters, of maternity. Her colour is yellow. This god of beauty is represented by Our Lady of Charity.

Oyansa - Known as *Oyá* or *Yansa*. This orisha rules the lightning bolt and the cemetery. A brave warrior, she accompanies her lover *Changó* in battle. Represented by St Theresa and Our Lady of the Presentation of Our Lord (formerly known as Our Lady of Candlemas).

paisano - friend, comrade, countryman

paleros - People who work with trees (known as *palos*) that have the power to do good or evil. According to some of the *paleros* I have spoken to, those initiated into this profession (known as *pinos nuevos* - new pines) have their backs, their foreheads and their breasts marked with cuts shaped like crosses. They are also obliged to swallow *la chamba* - a mixture of dust, earth from a cemetery, bones of the dead, etc. *Paleros* work with corpses that they disinter in the cemetery. They also work with the devil.

plantados - Political prisoners who refuse to submit to the 're-education' plan that is imposed in prisons.

santero - A Cuban witchdoctor or *Santería* priest.

Santería - An Afro-Cuban religion which emerged when slaves in Cuba were forced to adopt the Roman Catholic religion. Rather than lose their Nigerian Yoruba religion they modified it so as to make it appear more Christian. Thus, in *Santería*, Yoruba gods are identified with Christian saints. Possession by these powers, who will be able to help or protect the person possessed, is brought about through drumming and singing.

secret society made up of abacuás and ñáñigos - Founded in the XIX Century in Regla. Its sacred tree is the silk-cotton tree. It is said that this society was originally made up mainly of single black men who did not admit whites or mulattos as members. According to what some *abacuás* have told me, their sect insists on moral rectitude and a spirit of fraternity. However, in Cuba, around the 40's and 50's, stories of *ñáñigos* that stole white children in order to offer them up as sacrifices proliferated. As a result, this sect is greatly feared by people.

Sojuano - According to Victor, this is the name of an African deity represented by St Lazarus. It has proved impossible to verify this information. No-one has heard of this deity. The most common representation of St Lazarus is *Babalú Ayé*, an orisha who shows off his deformed body full of suppurating tumours. He cures those that suffer from these same ills.

tapiada - A totally closed punishment cell. May be a subterranean cellar.

the beat of a drum - It is said that in the beat of a drum - in its sound - is the voice of the saint. The *Iyabó* can offer a beating of the drums to the Saint. The *Iyabó* can also make an offering of coconuts, bananas, money, etc. to the sacred drums.

The Onceno Festival - was celebrated between the 27 July and the 5 August, 1978. An international youth festival which is celebrated in a different country each year. During the Onceno Festival the Law of Dangerousness was invoked to massive proportions in order to keep not only political dissidents but also those considered to be 'scum', 'antisocial' and 'hostile' in jail.

tupamuro - A cigarette made from mattress stuffing, threads from clothing, newspaper or any available material.

vida, mi vida - life; my life

volcano - A tin in which water is boiled. Two electric cables are used as an element.

Yemayá - The orisha who reigns over the sea, possessing all its wealth. *Yemayá* is represented by Our Lady of Regla. Her colour is blue.

Yoni; *Yoni* Land - The United States. An expression probably derived from the first name, Johnny.

Yuma - The United States

yuma clothes - Clothes from the United States.